B
IS   YS

sweatdrop
ORIGINAL UK MANGA STUDIOS
www.sweatdrop.com

BLUE
IS FOR BOYS

editor / Selina Dean
assisted by / Hayden Scott-Baron
cover design / Hayden Scott-Baron
cover image / Hayden Scott-Baron
rear cover image / Laura Watton

comics contributed by /
Sam Brown
Hayden Scott-Baron
Rik Nicol
Sarah Burgess
Hannah Saunders
Laura Watton
Stephanie Drewett
Selina Dean
Vanessa Wells

with additional writing by /
Mary Beaird
Fehed Said

assistance and retouch by /
Sam Brown
Laura Watton
Selina Dean

All works © 2005 their respective authors. All rights reserved. No portion of this book may be reproduced or transmitted in any form or by any means without permission from the copyright holders.

Published by Sweatdrop Studios
www.sweatdrop.com

ISBN 978-1-905038-08-4

Printed in the UK
First printing, October 2006

foreword

By Paul Gravett

You could say shonen manga were what first captivated me about Japanese comics. Back in 1980, on my lunch-hour escape from a mundane office job, I had discovered next to St. Paul's cathedral a whole bookshop heaving with books, magazines and comics piled high from Japan. Where should I start? Their import prices were not cheap and all the paperbacks were sealed tight in plastic, keeping their contents tantalisingly secret. But the magazines had only a protective band around them, so you could peek inside if you were careful, though the staff clearly did not approve.

In the end, dizzy with choice, I plumped for a copy of Kodansha's long-running Shonen Magazine, 170 yen for 362 pages, its spine over one inch thick, numbered 17, which I worked out meant the 17th week of the year, so dated April 20th. Fascinated, I must have looked at this extraordinary artefact dozens of times, losing myself in an explosive action panel, speedlines pulsating on the eye like Op Art, and jagged sound effects shrieking, or a sudden extreme caricatured face, fanged and demonic. I'd never seen panels bleeding off the edges of the page, as if their bursting power could not be contained inside any frame. Sheer energy and exuberance, sometimes manic, are key shonen qualities.

My Shonen Magazine has become faded, dog-eared, fragile, but I'd never throw it away. Digging it out again, breathing in its inky, musty bouquet, it all comes back. Looking closer, in places you can see the printing has struck the thin newsprint so heavily, the line art almost cuts into the paper like an etching. There's no full colour inside, aside from ads, but Go Nagai's fantastical grotesques and Takao Yaguchi's fishing thrills shimmer, rich and subtle, in their washes of blue half-tones.

There's also room for mood and sentiment. Another favourite was the small, moody youngster I'm Teppei, with his one thick continuous eyebrow and X-shaped scar across his nose. Tetsuya Chiba fills this episode about a hike with mates in the wintry countryside with wonderful details: melting icicles, relaxing with games and guitar-playing inside their cabin, towering mountains, the first flowers poking through snow. Much of the appeal of shonen manga is rooting for the little guy, the underdog, the misfit, who eventually overcomes obstacles and fulfils his dreams. They're stories of pluck and spirit to inspire anyone, of any age or sex..

Fast forward to 2006, and manga have spread to Britain so successfully, that they have pollinated a fresh generation of British talents. I invite you to read and enjoy their anthology of shonen manga. You'll find that these promising new voices are working in this genre's varied styles and traditions, building on them and also developing their own.

Nicknamed "The Man at the Crossroads", Paul Gravett co-founded Escape, the influential 1980s British comics magazine, with Peter Stanbury and directed The Cartoon Art Trust's museum in its first gallery premises in the 1990s. An author, exhibition curator, lecturer and broadcaster, he has written the best-selling book Manga: Sixty Years of Japanese Comics, published in eight languages so far, directs the Comica festival at London's ICA, is a journalist for The Telegraph, Independent, Guardian, Dazed & Confused and Comics International, and consultant for TV documentaries about comics for The South Bank Show, BBC and Discovery Channel.

www.paulgravett.com
www.greatbritishcomics.com

preface

When we were coming up with the concept for this book, and its partner volume, *'Pink is for Girls'*, we couldn't have predicted how much hard work would be required. Not just the editorial work to put together two books at once, but from everyone, producing comics to fill what is, when combined as a pair, the largest Sweatdrop anthology yet.

The idea was too interesting to not follow through: to create two books, one for boys and one for girls, which while closely intertwined, explore the differences between shonen and shojo manga. In manga the differences between the genders runs deeper than simply tastes in genre – as girls sit down to read science fiction comics and boys buy volume upon volume of romance comics. Traditionally, one would expect it to be the other way around; certainly in this country people are brought up to believe that girls should be reading about ponies and kittens, and boys should be reading comics about the antics of delinquents. Yet in manga, we find every taste catered for, whether you're a boy or girl doesn't limit the type of story you can read.

Though the content found in manga transcends stereotypes, there are certain innate qualities and differences between manga for boys and manga for girls. Whether it's the literal verses the metaphorical, speedlines verses sparkles, or just a different perspective, shonen manga is distinctly boyish and shojo is distinctly girlish. In this volume, you will find nine stories for boys, each of which has a companion story in *'Pink is for Girls'*. The comics can be enjoyed alone, or with their partnered story.

We hope you like our book, whether you are a boy or a girl!

5

contents

7	**Alive in Triumph** Sam Brown
19	**Two Halves: Blue Seas** Hayden Scott-Baron
37	**Quest for Chenezzar** Rik Nicol
49	**Unmade Melody** Sarah Burgess
65	**Angel's Game: Steel Destrier** Hannah Saunders, Mary Beaird
77	**Steaming** Laura Watton
87	**Rotten** Stephanie Drewett, Fehed Said
103	**Super Brother** Selina Dean
119	**Transmutation** Vanessa Wells, Selina Dean

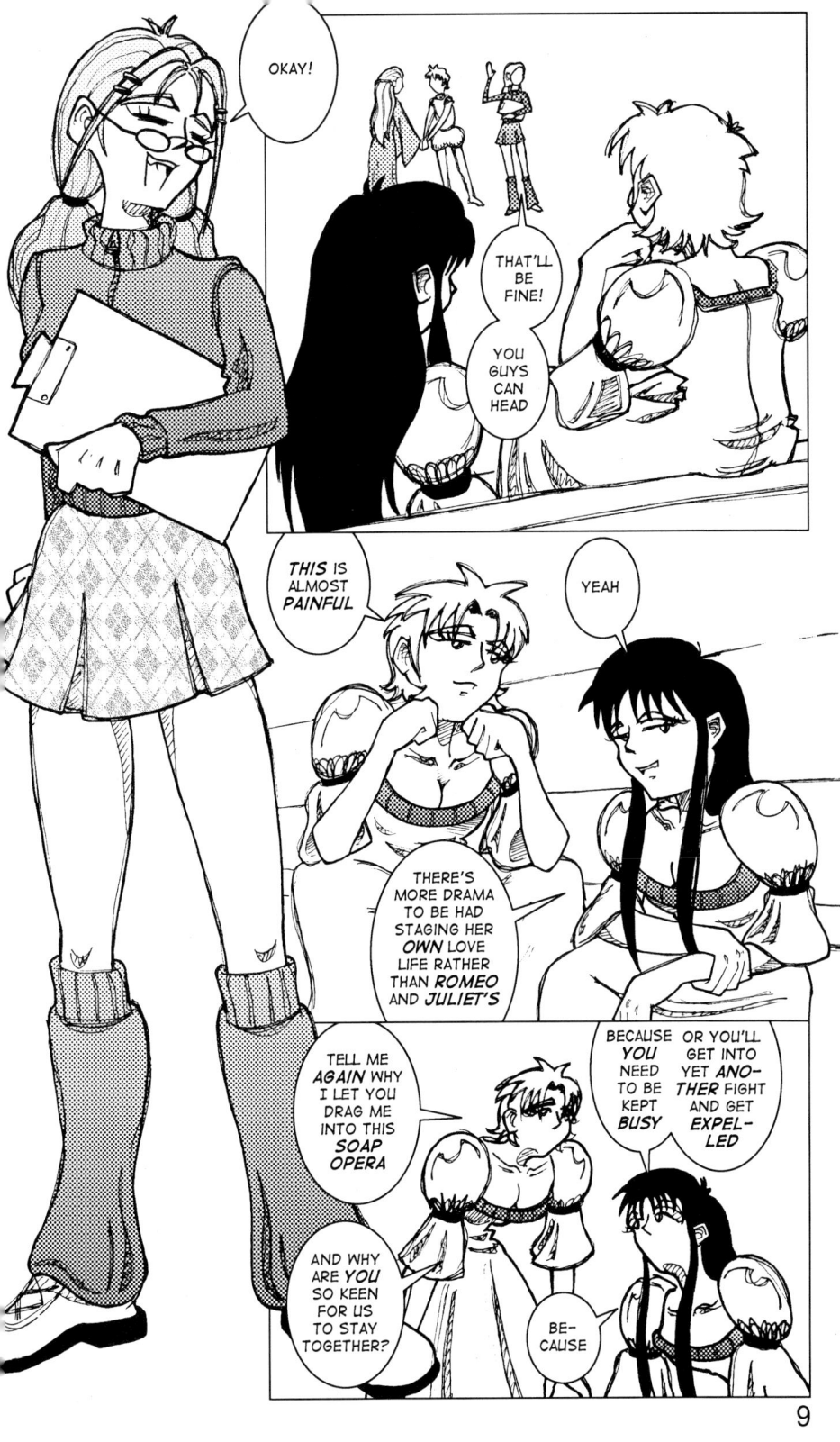

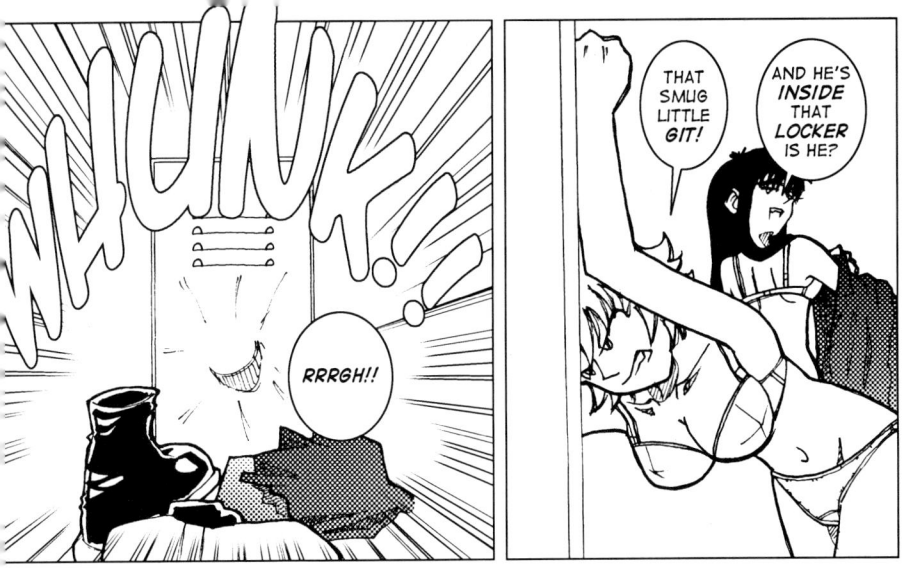

story & artwork by
Hayden Scott-Baron (aka Dock)

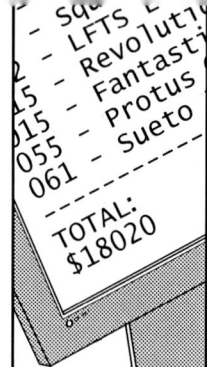

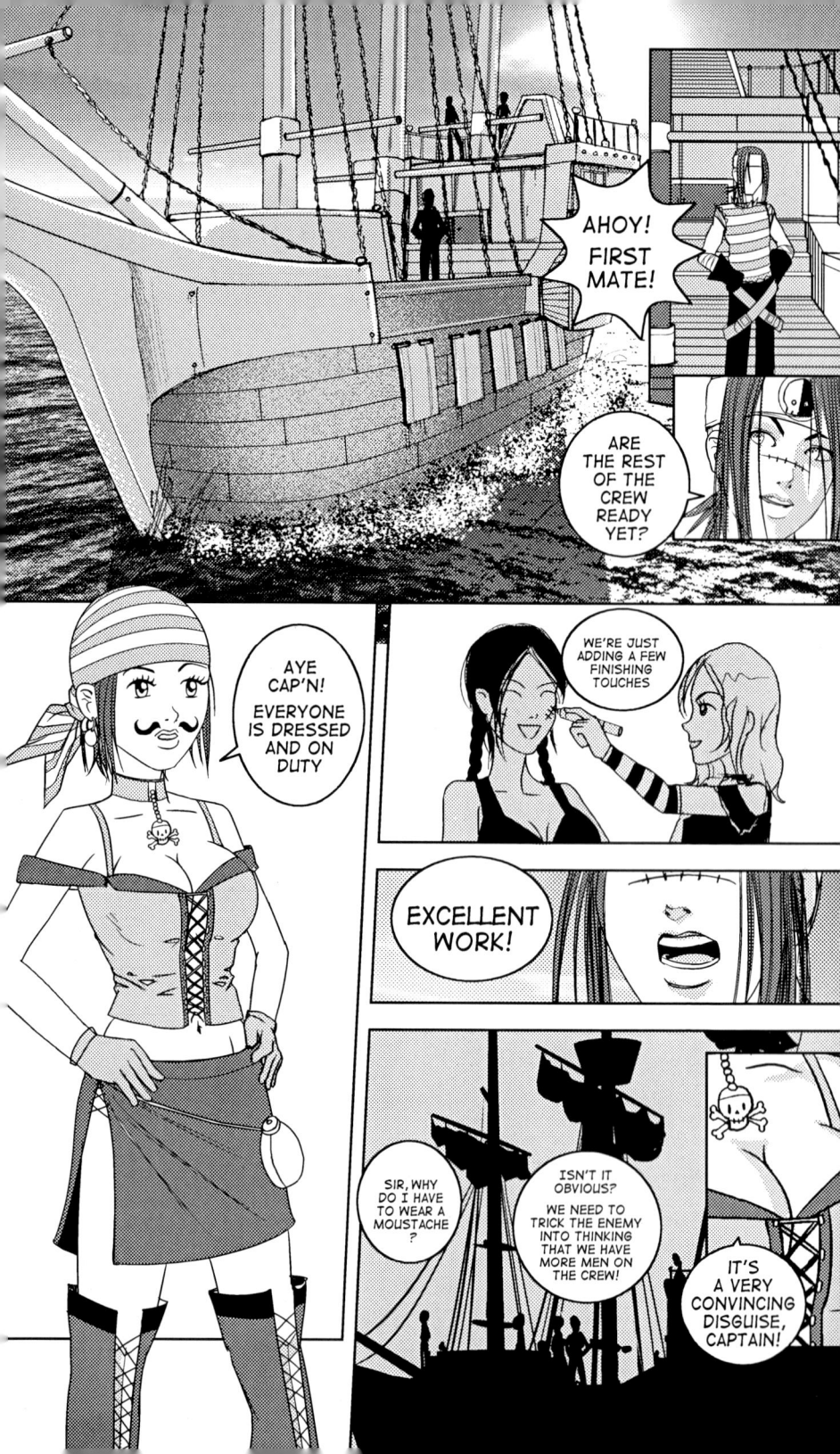

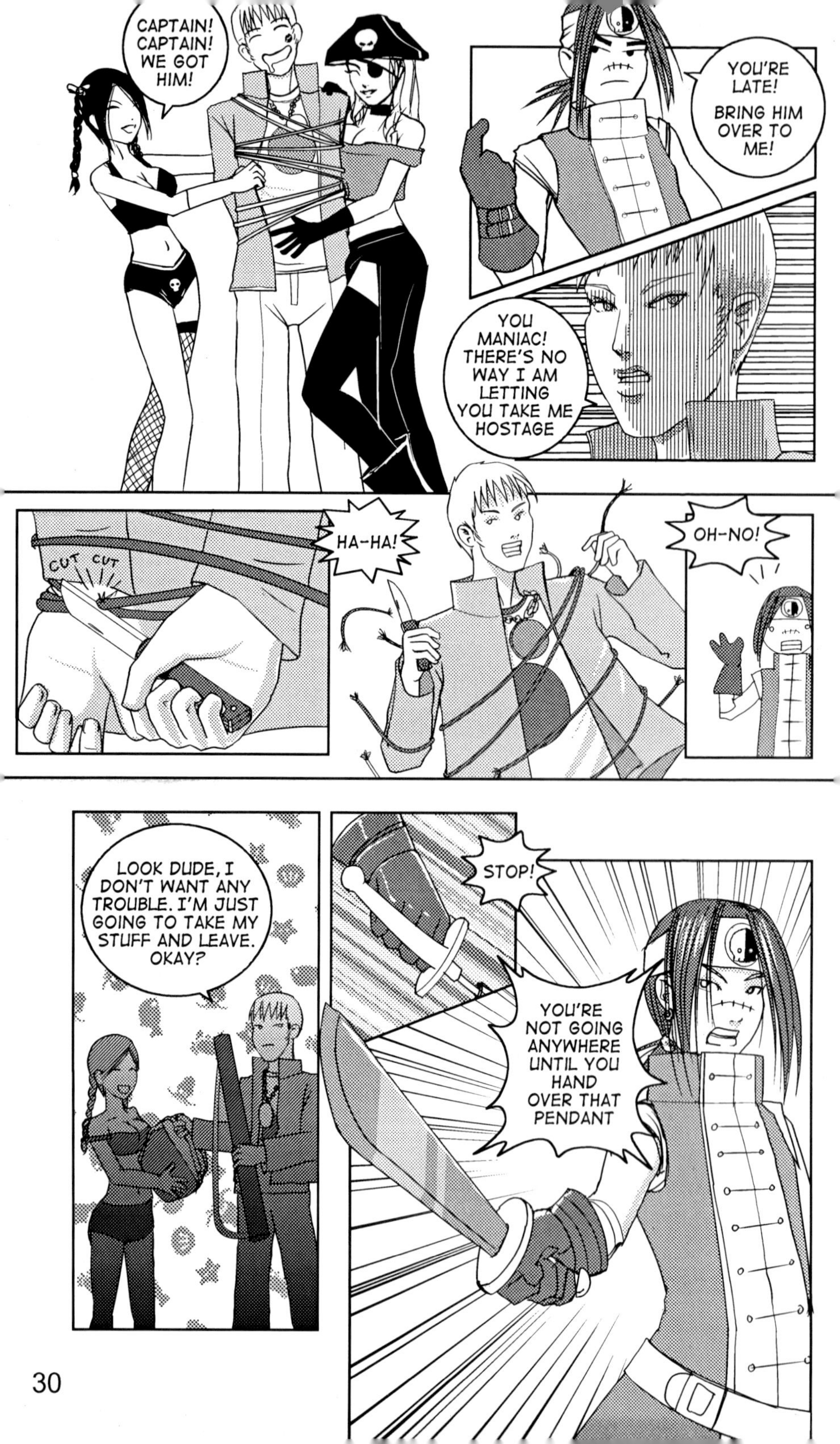

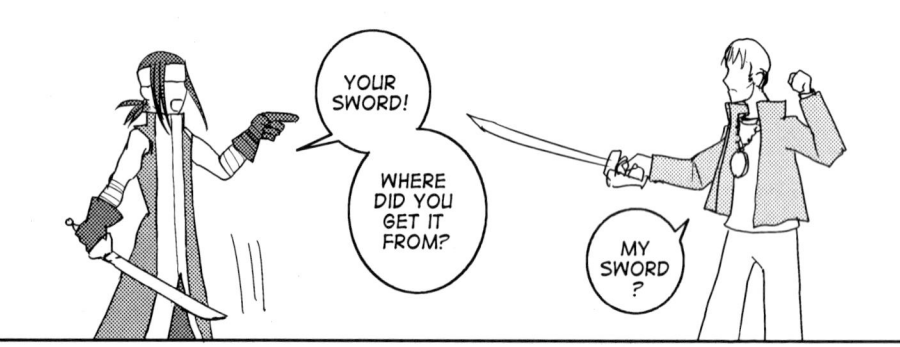

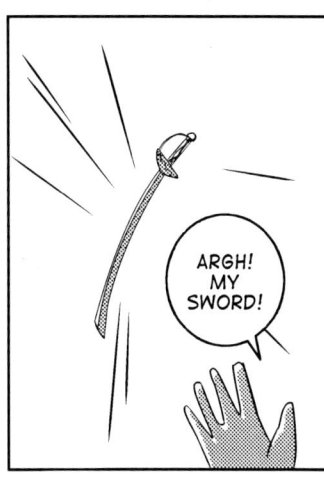

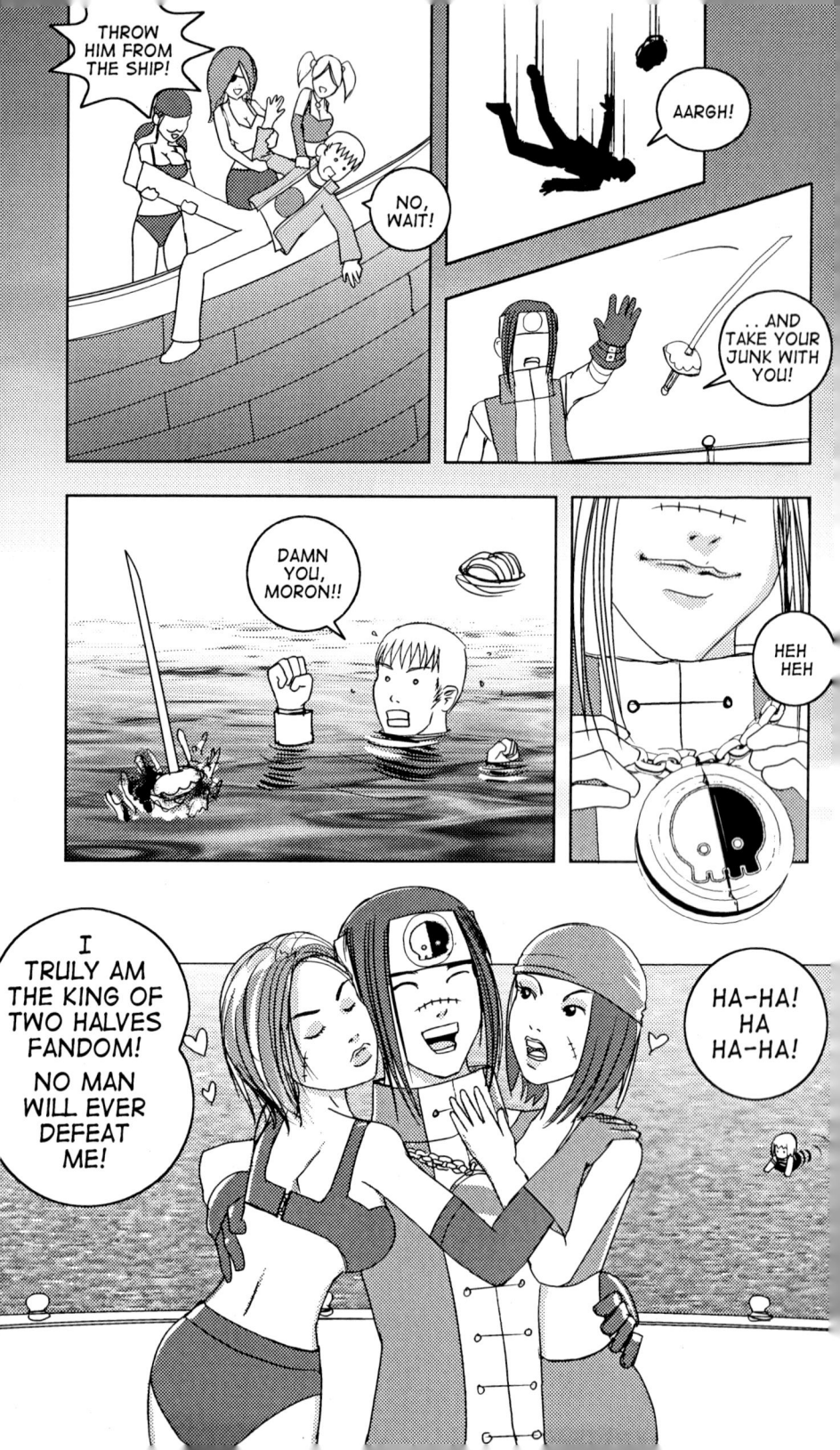

Quest for Chenezzar

ART & DIALOGUE BY RIK NICOL
CONCEPT BY SONIA LEONG

LORD CARMICHAEL, I'M GLAD YOU CAME. SADLY I FEAR THIS OUR LAST MEETING. I MUST APOLOGISE FOR ENDANGERING YOU BY ASKING YOU HERE.
I WOULD GLADLY TREAD THE PATH OF PERIL TO SERVE YOU, KING SIRIUS.
BUT I DO NOT UNDERSTAND... I HAVE BEEN TOLD YOU ARE TO RECOVER.
I SUSPECT WE BOTH KNOW SALAZAR WILL NOT AFFORD ME SUCH CONVENIENCE. BEING MY BROTHER, HE STANDS TO GAIN A GREAT DEAL, AND IT WOULD SEEM I HAVE FALLEN VICTIM TO HIS SCHEMING.
YOU WARNED ME OF HIM ONCE, BUT I WAS A FOOL. I DON'T DESERVE TO ASK OF YOU A FINAL REQUEST, BUT TIME IS RUNNING OUT AND THE OTHERS HAVE ALREADY FLOCKED TO SALAZAR'S SIDE...

AS YOU KNOW, QUEEN CADENZA (MAY SHE REST IN PEACE)... DIED DURING CHILDBIRTH.
ARGH! IT HURTS SO MUCH!
CADENZA!
...I WAS INFORMED OUR BEAUTIFUL DAUGHTER, SONATINA, DIDN'T MAKE THE NIGHT.
...HOWEVER, IT HAS BECOME CLEAR SHE WAS LIKELY TAKEN TO ARGALIA DURING THE CHAOS.
YOU *MUST* FIND HER... THE TRUE HEIR TO THE THRONE.

GOING SOMEWHERE, LORD CARMICHAEL? I'M AFRAID I HAVE A PRESSING NEED FOR YOU IN THE LOWER CHAMBERS.
SALAZAR! YOU ARE NOT THE KING AND I SHALL NOT HEED YOUR ORDERS!
OH THAT OLD FOOL DIED SHORTLY AFTER YOUR LITTLE CHAT, SO I'M AFRAID I REALLY *AM* YOUR KING. I ASK OF YOU... WILL YOU OBEY MY RULE? IT REALLY WOULD BE A SHAME TO WITNESS ANOTHER DEATH SO SOON...
UNTIL THE CORONATION, YOU ARE BUT A WORM AND I YIELD TO NO SUCH CREATURE.

VERY WELL, VERY WELL. BEST OF LUCK WITH YOUR LITTLE QUEST. I DO SINCERELY HOPE NO CALAMITIES BEFALL YOUR JOURNEY...
...
AHA!
ARGH!

KICK

MOST DARING...

STAB!
KICK!
YOU FIGHT AS FOOLISH AS YOU LOOK. I WILL NOT BE STOPPED BY COWARDLY ASSASSINS, MUCH LESS COWARDLY ASSASSINS IN FANCY DRESS.

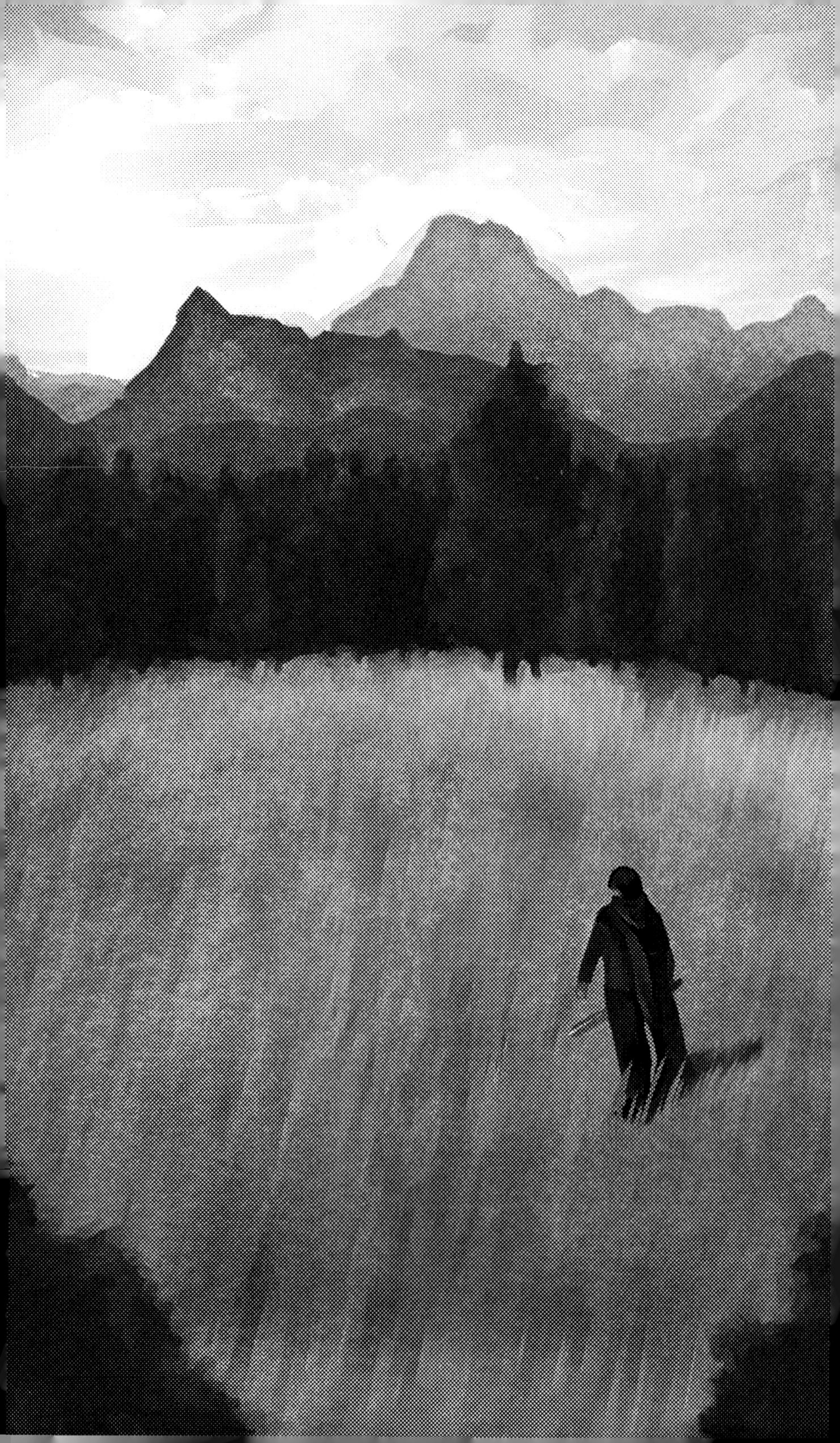

RUSTLE RUSTLE

...I KNOW YOU'RE THERE

...LET'S GET THIS OVER WITH.

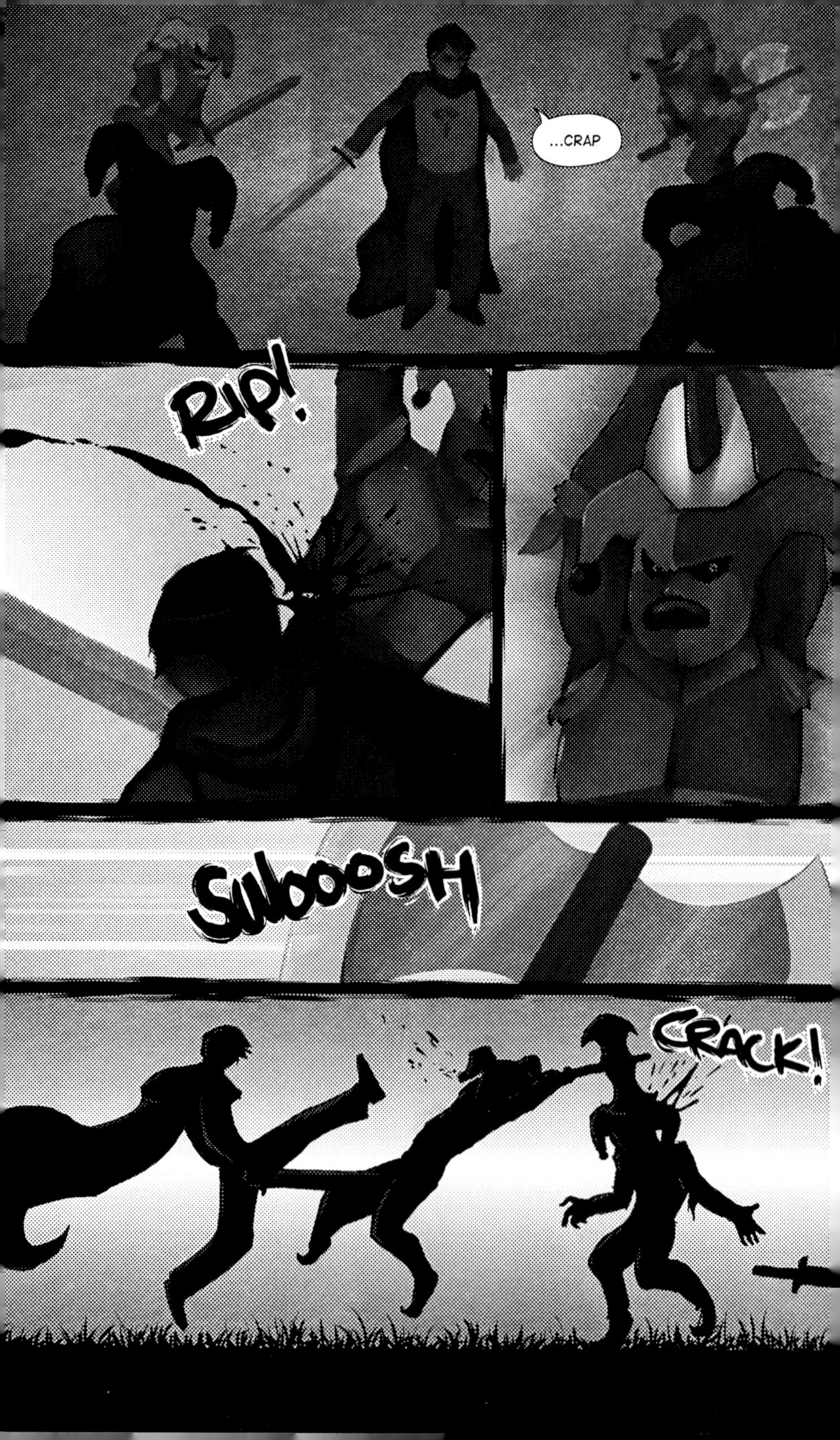
...CRAP
RIP!
SWOOOSH
CRACK!

STAB!

COUGH

...UGH
NOT FAR NOW...
OH MY, YOU'RE BLEEDING! LET ME HELP YOU!
CADENZA!?
THUD!

IT'S BEEN ONE YEAR...

SINCE THAT EVENT.

AND NOW HE IS BACK

I REMEMBER...

Unmade Melody

Pencils and scripting
 - Sarah Burgess

Story, edits and letters
 - Morag Lewis

Inks and tone
 - Laura Watton

YES! IT'S THE AUDITION FOR THE SCHOOL CONCERT!

I'VE BEEN PRACTISING ALL WEEK..

I WORKED SO HARD, I'LL WIN FOR SURE!
HMMM... EVERYONE SURE IS NERVOUS.
BAD PLAYING.

... BUT THAT GUY...
WHERE HAVE I SEEN HIM?.... ... HE'S SO CALM.
IT'S LIKE HE DOESN'T CARE... LIKE HE HASN'T TRIED AT ALL.
PEOPLE LIKE THAT ANNOY ME.

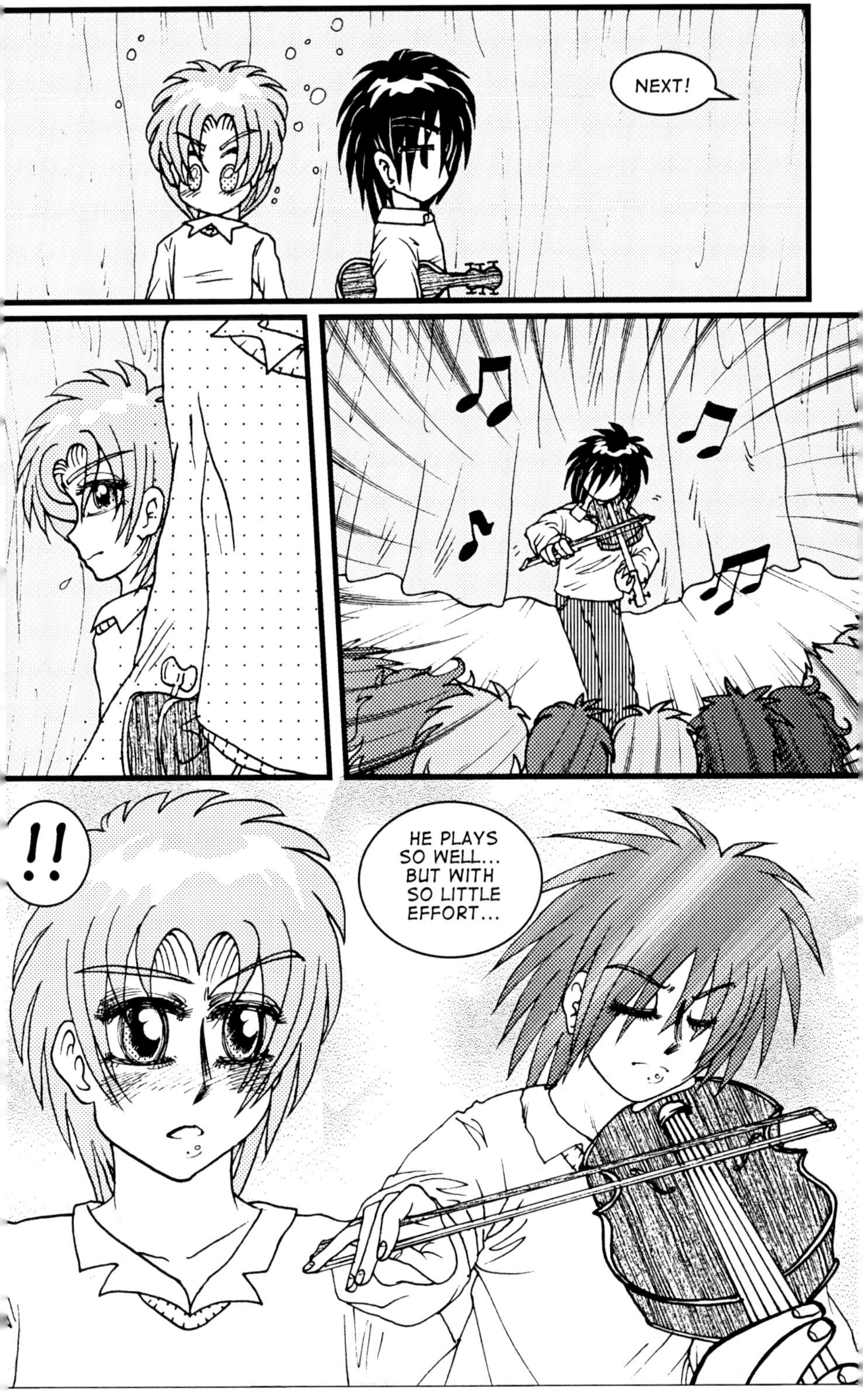
NEXT!
!!
HE PLAYS SO WELL... BUT WITH SO LITTLE EFFORT...

WOW!
EXCELLENT
YOU GET THE PART.
?!
... THANKS.
H...
HOW COULD THIS HAPPEN?!
HE DOESN'T EVEN CARE AND THEY GAVE HIM THE PART??!!
I NEVER GOT A CHANCE...
- AT LEAST I AM GOOD AT SOMETHING ELSE.

WOW!!
ISN'T HE SO COOL?!
THAT'S DAN -
HYAH!!
HE'S THE BEST AT NINJUTSU IN OUR CLASS

YAH!!

IT'S THAT GUY!

WHAT'S HIS NAME?

THAT'S ALISTAIR.

HE'S ALMOST AS GOOD AS YOU.

ALISTAIR...
I'LL SHOW YOU FOR RUINING MY HARD WORK.
HEY!
?
?
WHAT?
I CHALLENGE YOU TO A FIGHT!
ALL RIGHT
YAAAAAAH!!!
HA!!
!!

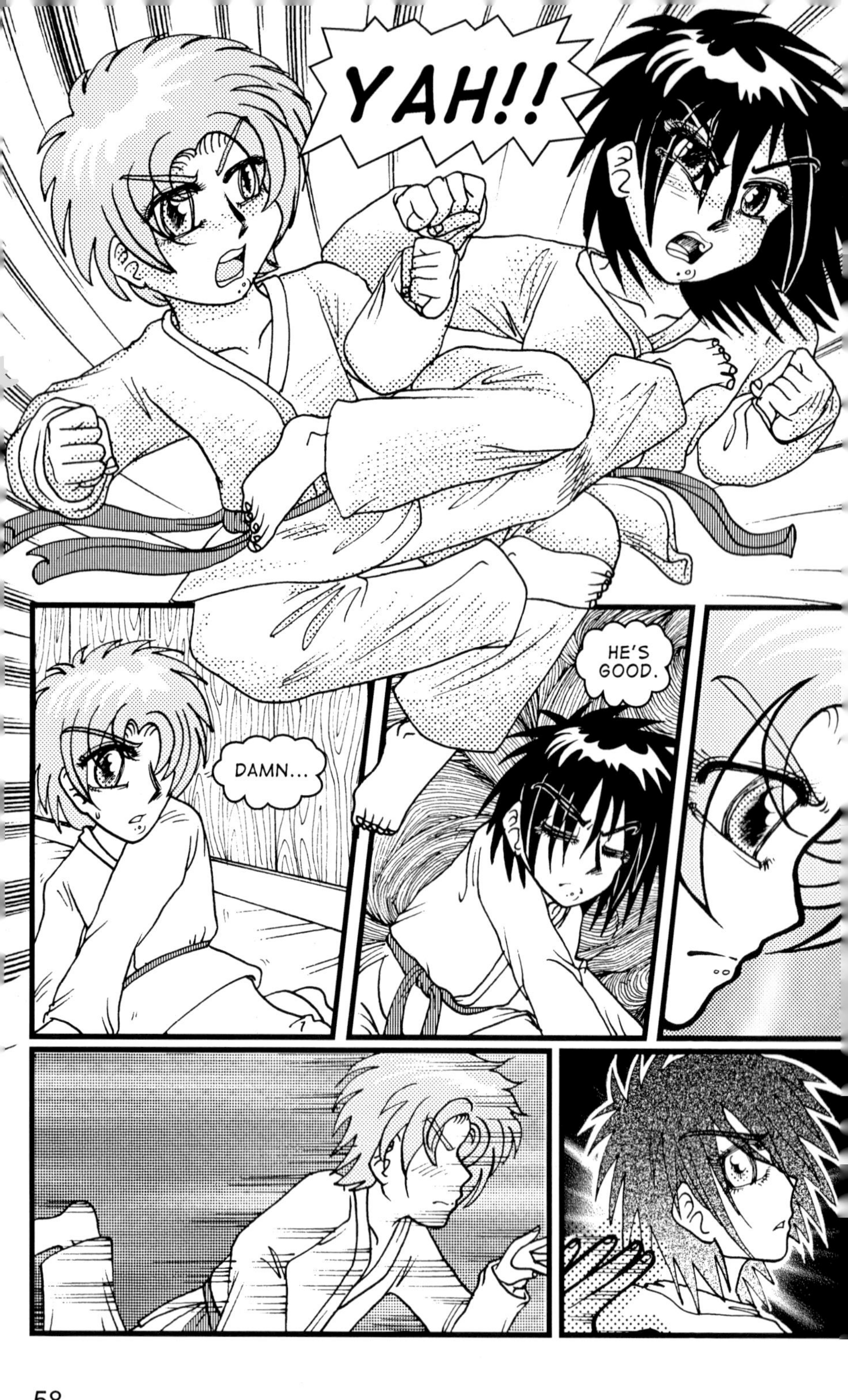
YAH!!!
HE'S GOOD.
DAMN...

I WIN!

... FINE.

WHY...

... WHY IS HE SO COLD?

HE NEVER [H]AS FEELINGS... [O]UR SKILLS WERE MATCHED.

I WANT TO SEE HIM FEEL...

... I NEED TO BEAT HIM PROPERLY... AND I WILL.

THAT MUSIC...
ALISTAIR...
ALL HIS FEELINGS... IN THE MUSIC?
... I'LL DEFEAT YOU PROPERLY...

ALISTAIR.
ALISTAIR...
?
HUH?
THIS TIME...
I WILL DEFEAT YOU PROPERLY!
WHA...?
YOU DO THINGS WITH NO EFFORT OR WORK -
WHILE OTHERS WORK HARD AND GAIN NOTHING!

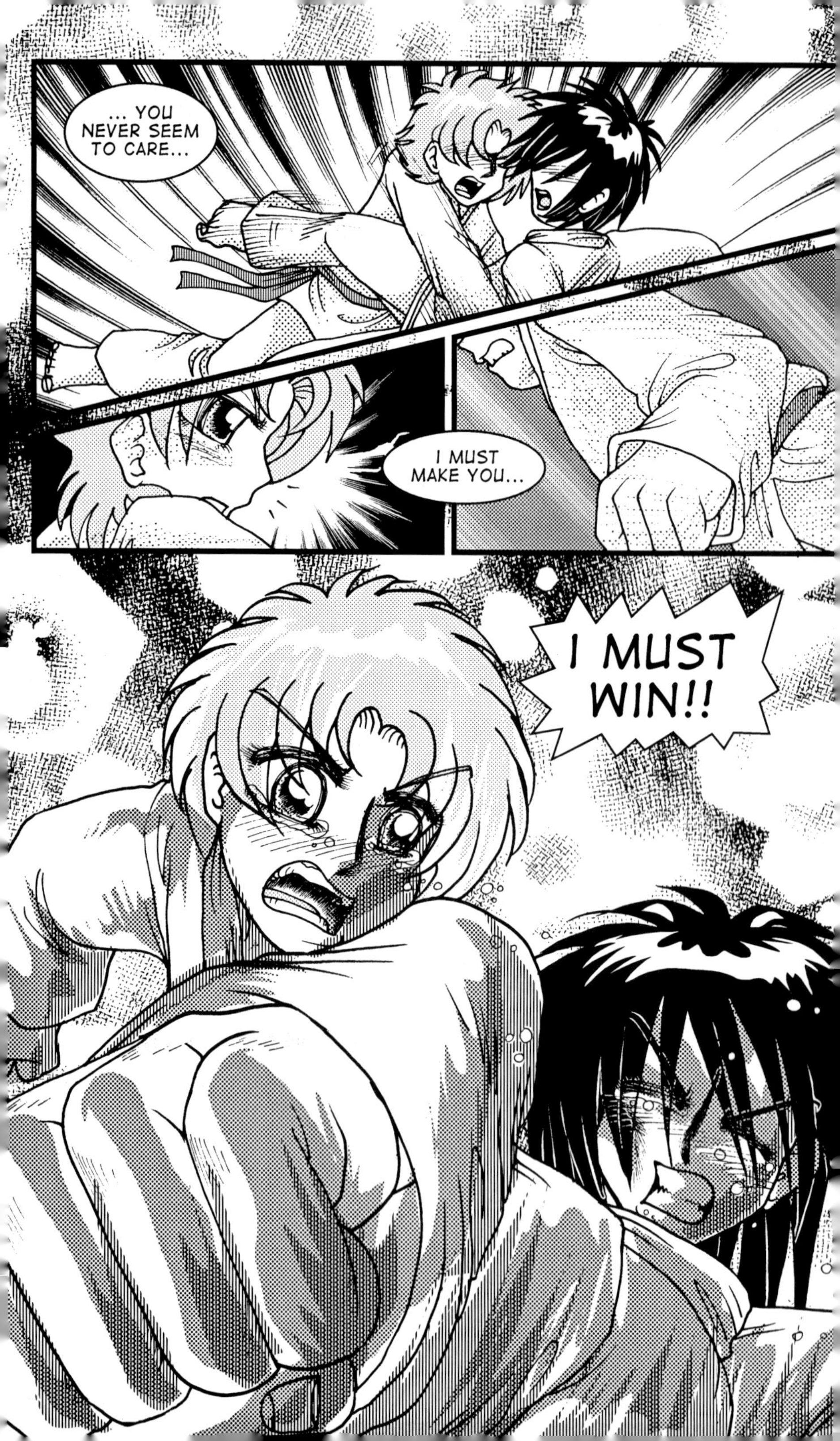
... YOU NEVER SEEM TO CARE...
I MUST MAKE YOU...
I MUST WIN!!

YES!!
NOW YOU SEE -
ALISTAIR!
!!
HOSPITAL
MRS FARRELL.
W - WHAT?
I'M AFRAID HIS HEARING HAS BEEN IRREPARABLY DAMAGED.
... A POWERFUL IMPACT TO THE BACK OF HIS HEAD.
DON'T YOU THINK IT'S A BIT HARSH, SAYING THAT OVER HIS HEAD?
PFFT. WHAT DOES HE KNOW?
IT'S NOT LIKE HE CAN HEAR US.

SO NOW HE'S RETURNED....
AFTER ALL THAT, HE'S STILL HERE.
HE NEVER EVEN SAID ANYTHING..
AS IF NOTHING HAPPENED.
HIS PRIDE WAS NOT BASED ON OTHER PEOPLE'S OPINIONS.
HE DID NOT RELY ON THEIR PRAISE.
I ONLY TOOK SATISFACTION IN MY TALENT IF OTHER PEOPLE RECOGNISED IT.
BUT NOW I SEE...
I DON'T NEED OTHER PEOPLE'S APPROVAL TO KNOW WHETHER I AM GOOD OR NOT...
... I AM VICTORIOUS BY MYSELF.
THANK YOU, ALISTAIR, AND...
I'M SORRY.

Angel's Game: Steel Destrier

Art by Hannah Saunders
Story by Mary Beaird

THE KNIGHT SLAYS THE DRAGON AND RESCUES HIS LOVE. IT'S AN OLD STORY. ANCIENT, IN FACT.

FROM THE TIME WHEN WE HAD THE BELIEFS AND FEARS OF CHILDREN, HUDDLED TOGETHER IN THE DARK FOR SAFETY...

WHISPERING TO EACH OTHER OF MONSTERS, AND THE FAERIE, AND MAGIC.

THEN WE GREW UP AND REJECTED THE SHADOW TALES IN FAVOUR OF FACT, SCIENCE AND LOGIC.

FINALLY WE ADVANCED FAR ENOUGH TO SPREAD OUR WINGS AND LEAVE THE CONFINES OF OUR TINY WORLD.

IRONIC TO FIND THAT THE MONSTERS AND MAGIC HAD BEEN OUT HERE ALL ALONG. PATIENTLY WAITING FOR US. IN THE DARK.

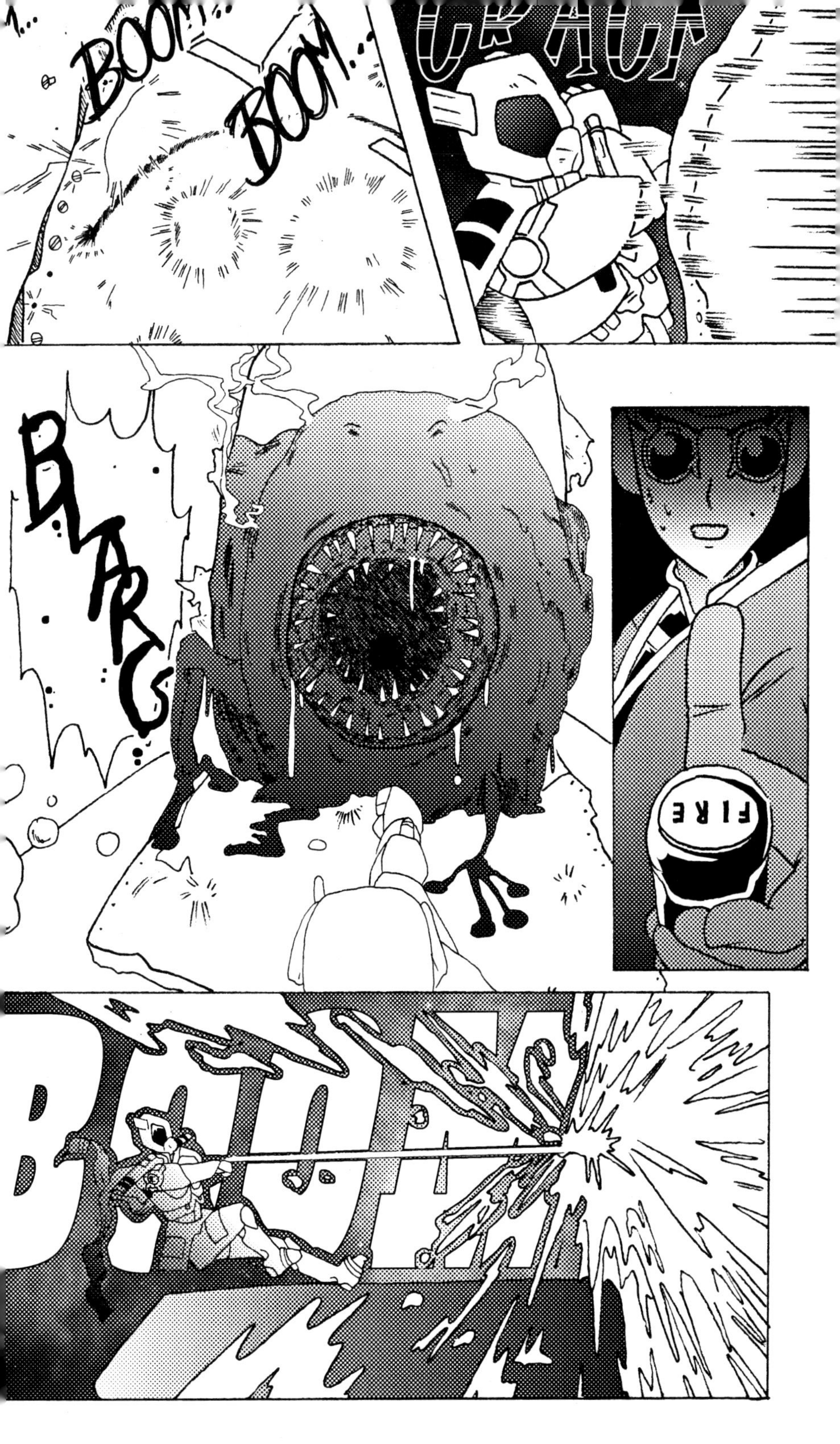

BOOM...
BOOM...
CRACK
BLARG
FIRE

FLIP

...

squelch

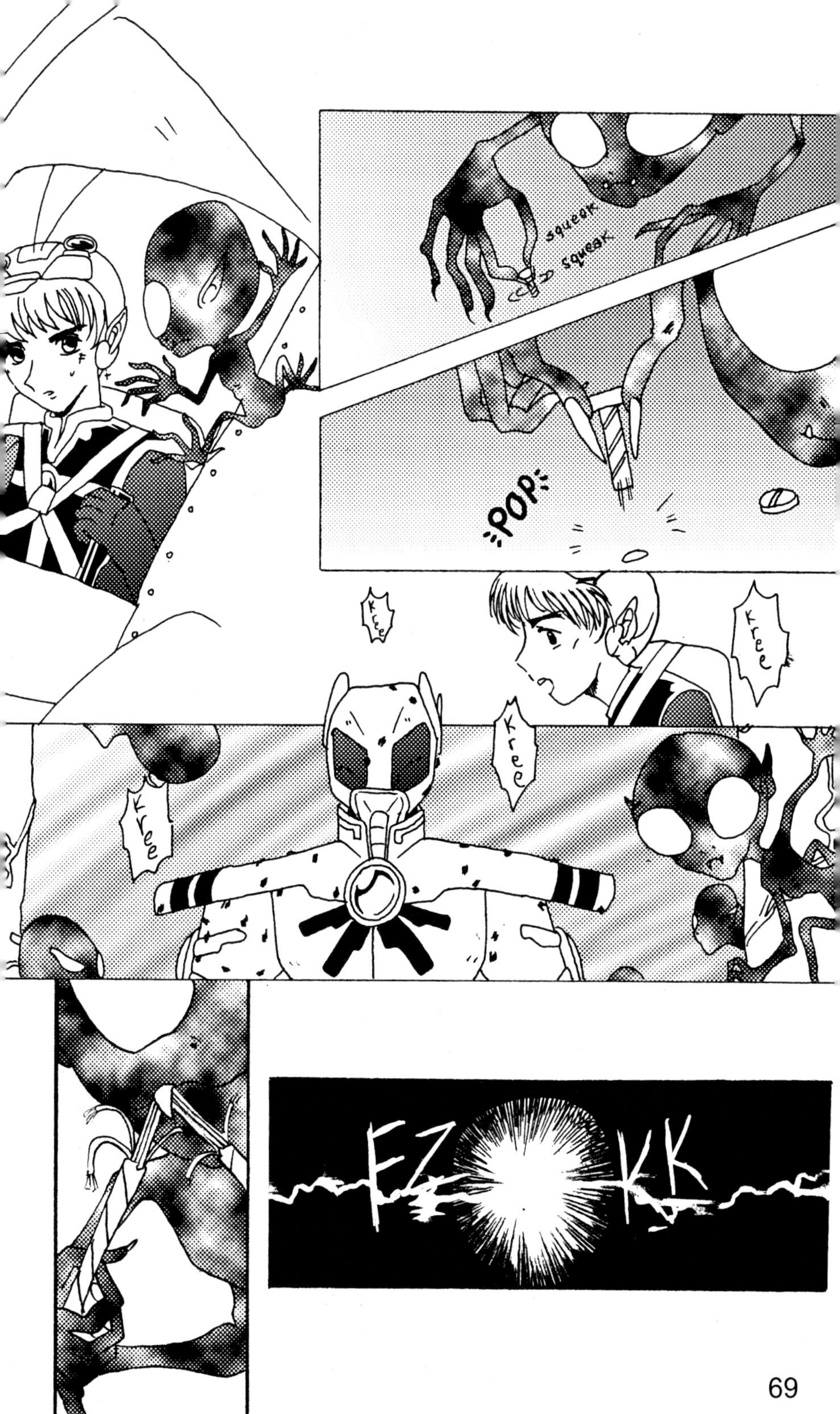
squeak
squeak
POP
Kree
Kree
Kree
Kree
FZ KK

=CHK=

VERMIN!!

BLAM

BLAM

BLAM BLAM

THIS IS GETTING **STUPID!**

beep Greetings, intruder. Please identify.
GREETINGS? INTRUDER? A STRANGE WELCOME!
IDENTIFICATION WING COMMANDER MARCUS 3595364, DEXIV.
AND WHO ARE YOU?
Designation Hamaliel. Station computer. Instructed to contact and advise.
BY WHOM?
Prisoners on Level 9.
ABOUT TIME! BUT *PRISONERS?!* HOW MANY ARE THERE?
There are currently two individuals in custody.
WELL, THAT'S GOING TO MAKE IT SNUG IN HERE!
I WONDER IF THERE'S A WORKING SHUTTLE-CRAFT IN THIS MAUSOLEUM!

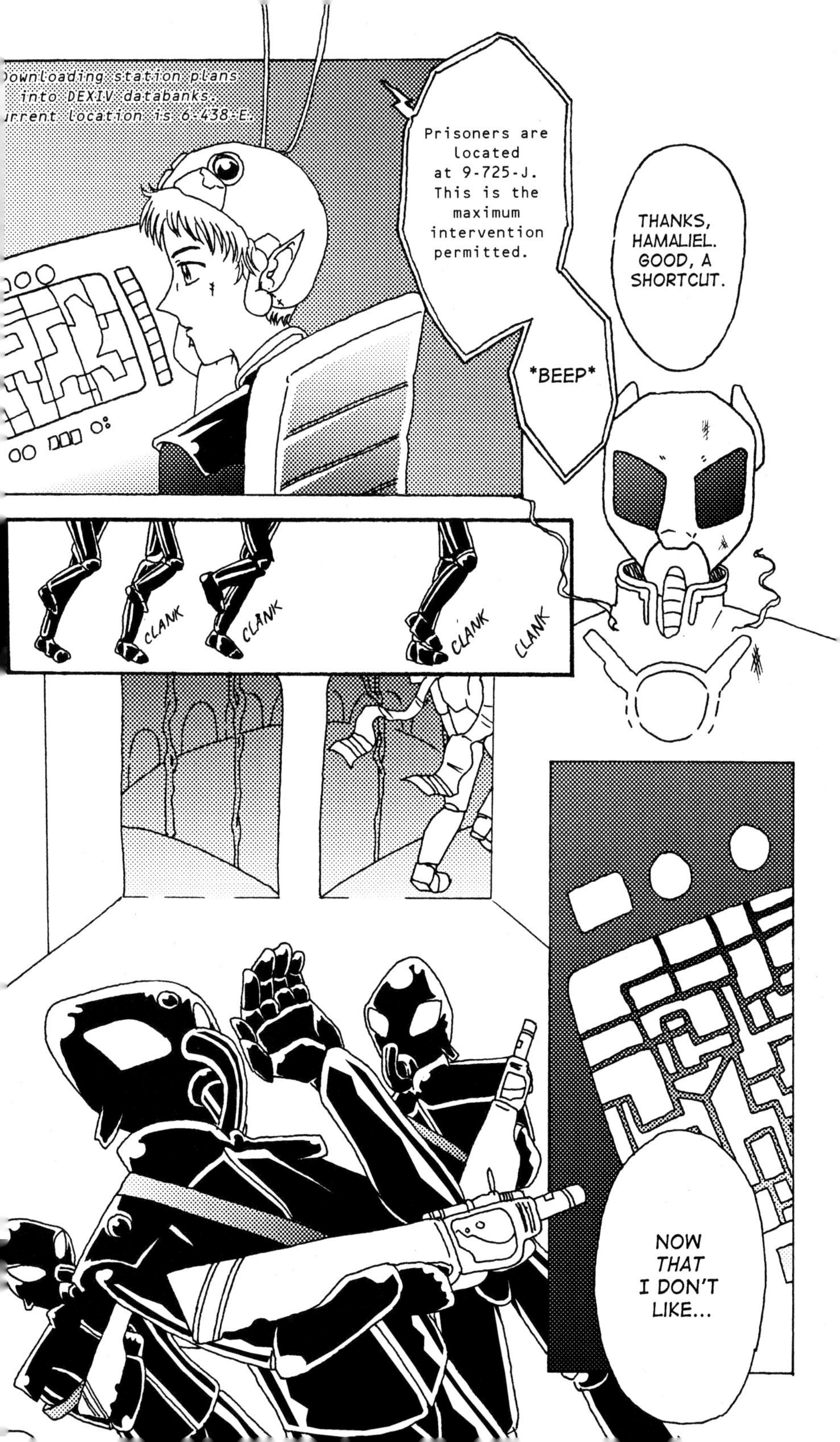

Downloading station plans into DEXIV databanks. Current location is 6-438-E.
Prisoners are located at 9-725-J. This is the maximum intervention permitted.
BEEP
THANKS, HAMALIEL. GOOD, A SHORTCUT.
CLANK
CLANK
CLANK
CLANK
NOW *THAT* I DON'T LIKE...

...BECAUSE IF THEY'RE NOT FOLLOWING IT MEANS...
...THERE'S SOMETHING WORSE UP AHEAD!!
GRAA
AALLL
KRK
!!
NOT ENOUGH POWER TO FRY IT...
...TOO ENCLOSED FOR CANNON, GRENADE OR LASER.
YOU CAN'T KILL IT NOW, SO SCARE IT OFF....
...THOSE ARE ITS EYES. THINK, MARCUS. YOU KNOW THIS.
IT LIVES IN THE DARK.
NO NOSE, SO HOW DOES IT HUNT?
OF COURSE!

P.A. MAXIMUM VOLUME. LOOP. AND FEEDBACK.

CLANG

VVVOOOO

!!

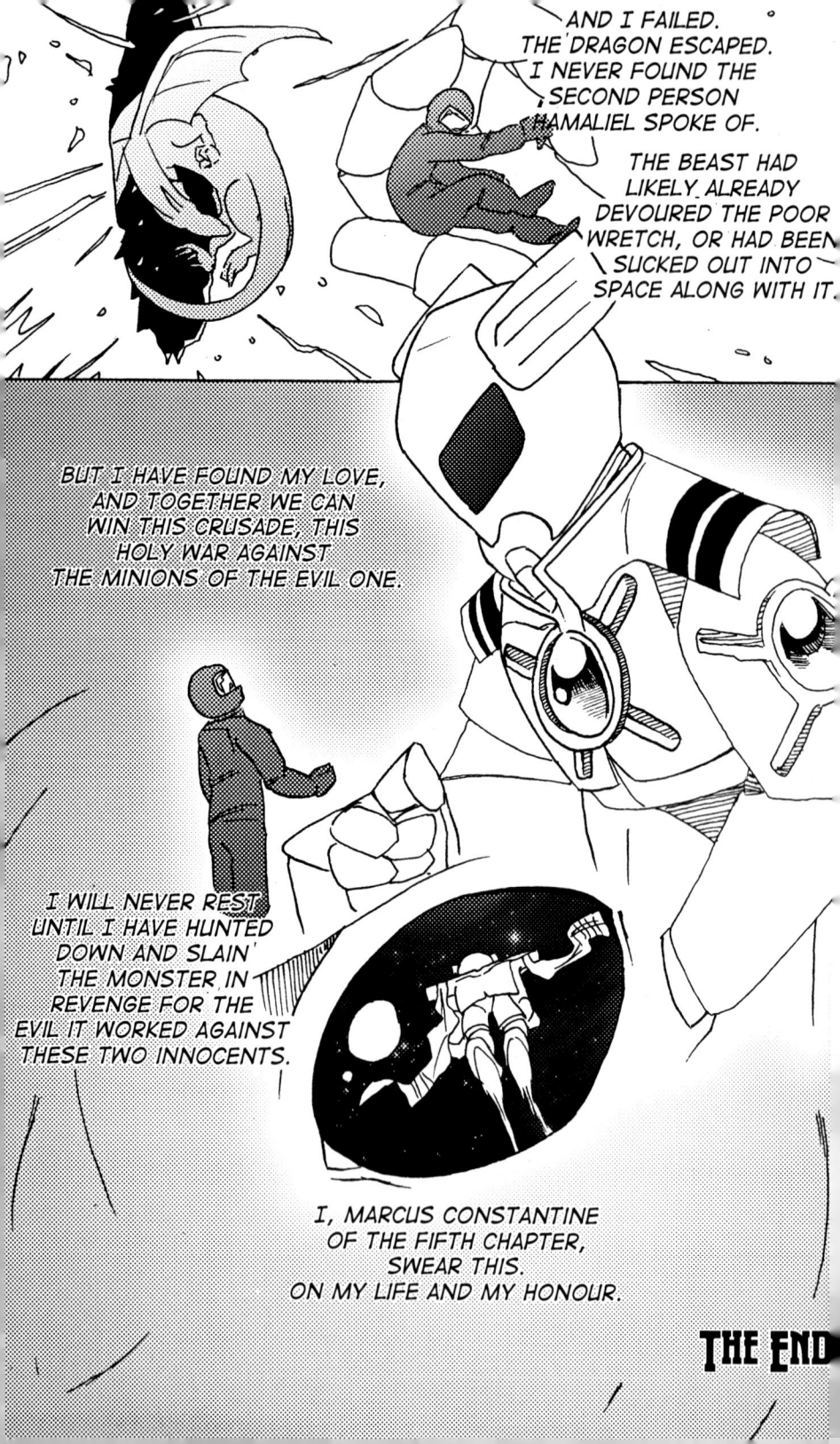

AND I FAILED. THE DRAGON ESCAPED. I NEVER FOUND THE SECOND PERSON HAMALIEL SPOKE OF.

THE BEAST HAD LIKELY ALREADY DEVOURED THE POOR WRETCH, OR HAD BEEN SUCKED OUT INTO SPACE ALONG WITH IT.

BUT I HAVE FOUND MY LOVE, AND TOGETHER WE CAN WIN THIS CRUSADE, THIS HOLY WAR AGAINST THE MINIONS OF THE EVIL ONE.

I WILL NEVER REST UNTIL I HAVE HUNTED DOWN AND SLAIN THE MONSTER IN REVENGE FOR THE EVIL IT WORKED AGAINST THESE TWO INNOCENTS.

I, MARCUS CONSTANTINE OF THE FIFTH CHAPTER, SWEAR THIS. ON MY LIFE AND MY HONOUR.

THE END

Steaming

Art: Laura Watton
Story: Aleister Kelman and Laura Watton

Mimes

SIGH

THE PERIL OF CREATIVE FATIGUE!!

....

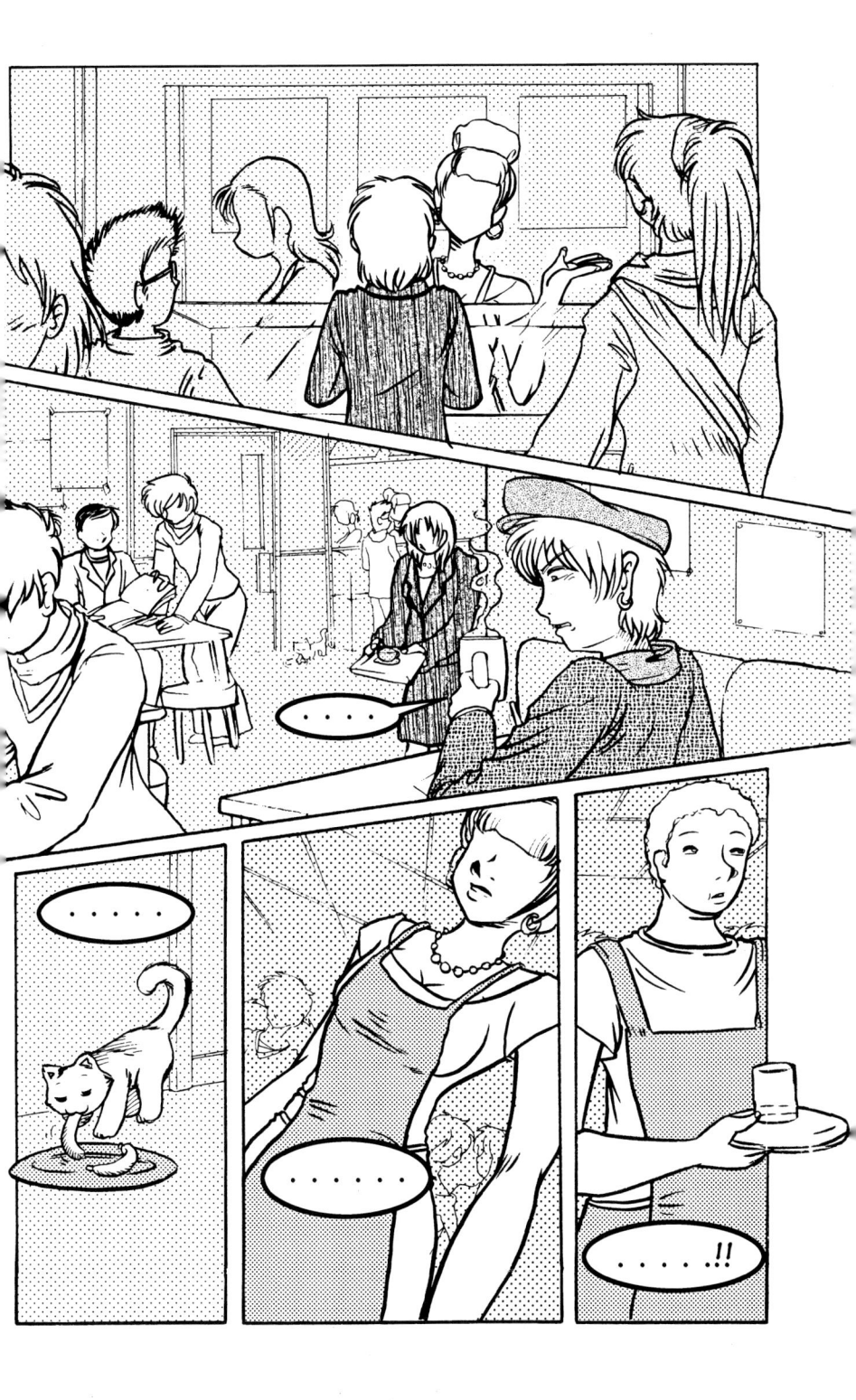

. . . .

. . . .

. . . . !!

...

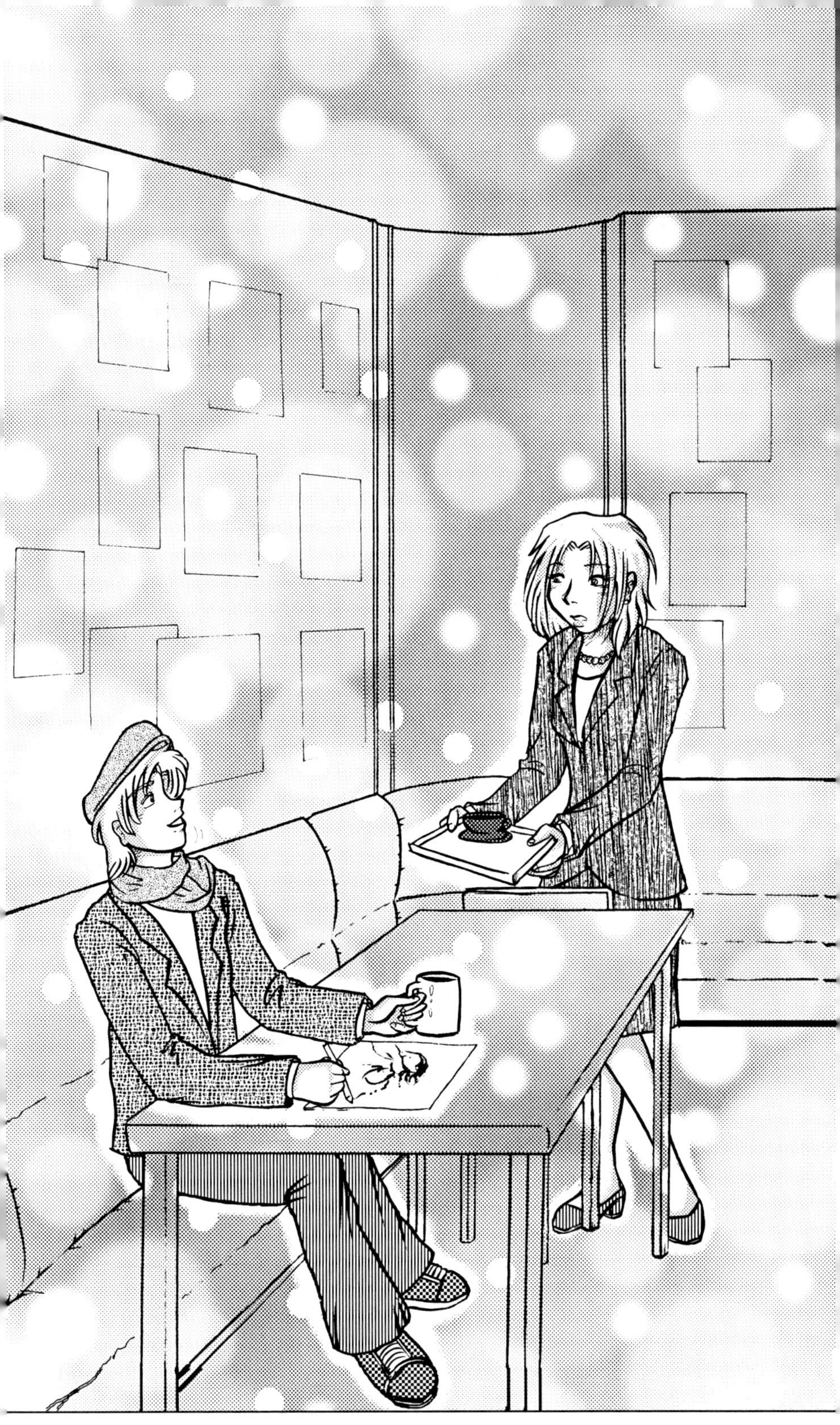

SO WEARY.

HOW HER SOUL MUST BE TORTURED...

SHE MAY BE A REAL *MINX* IN BED!

SHUDDER!

PERFECT!

WHAT MUST LIE BENEATH THAT OPRESSIVE UNIFORM?!

TURN

SHE'S SO NOVEL - LIKE SOMETHING OUT OF A MOVIE!
DON'T...
LOOK...
AWAY..!
I WONDER WHAT HER VOICE IS LIKE..?
THAT'S BETTER.
THE FAIRYTALE WORKER.
UNDERNEATH IT ALL...

EXQUISITE.

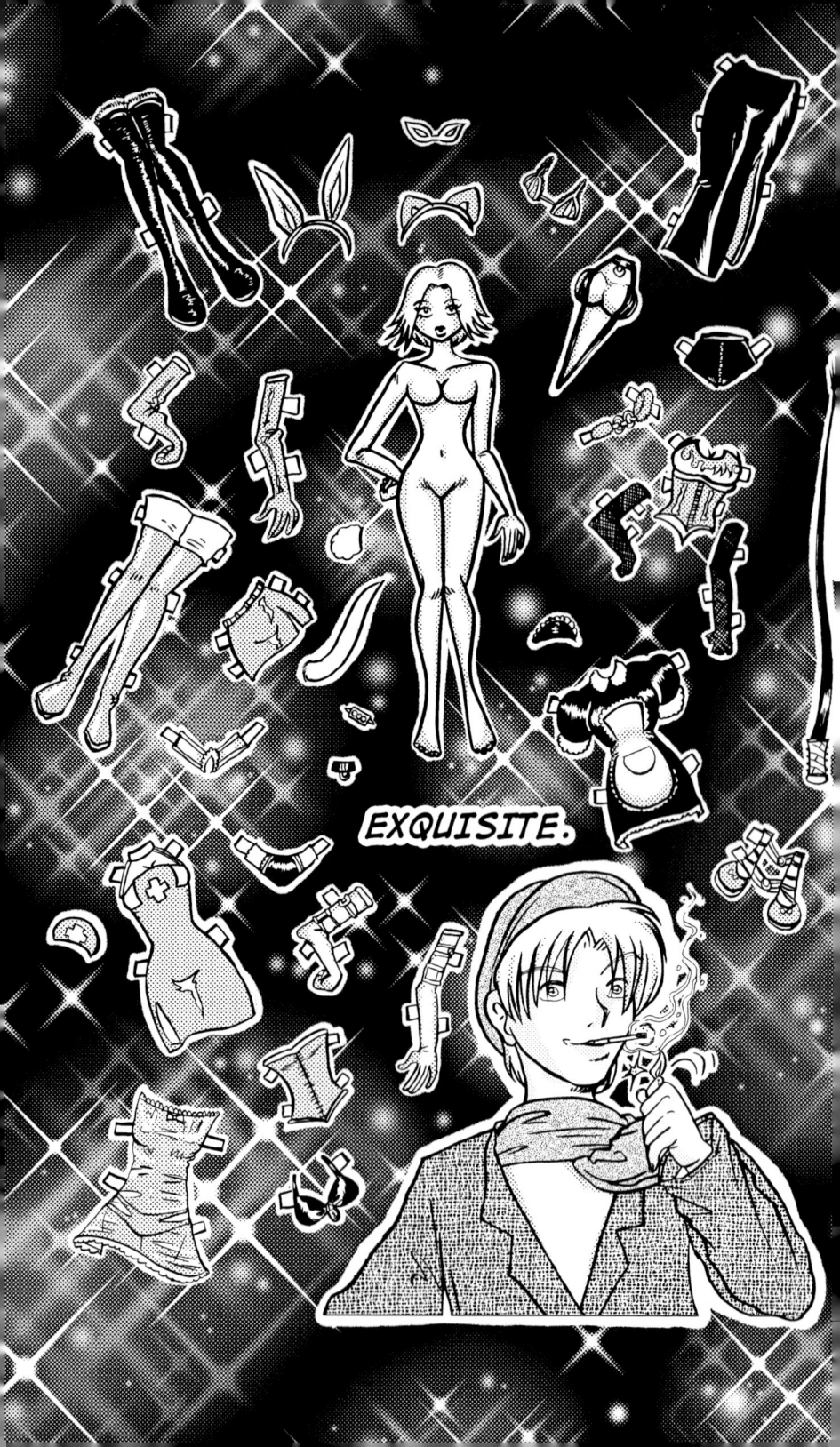

MAYBE SHE'S ACTUALLY REALLY HARSH UNDERNEATH...
SAUCY!
PERHAPS I COULD PAINT HER NUDE BY THE RIVERSIDE...
DECADENT!
MAYBE SHE'S
THE ONE.

HELLO.

HELLO...

THE END..?

Rotten

Story by Fred

Art by Stephanie Drewett

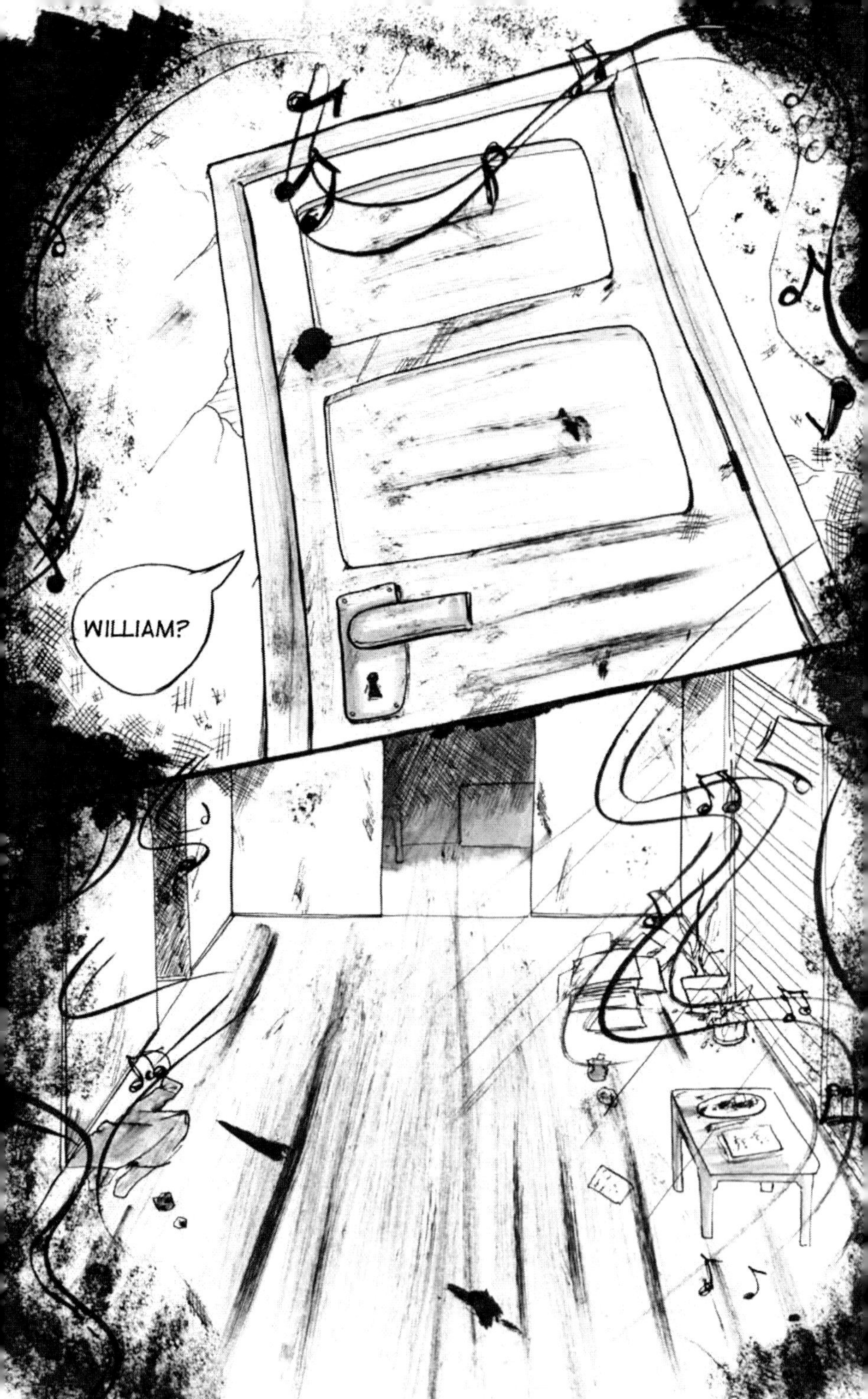
WILLIAM?

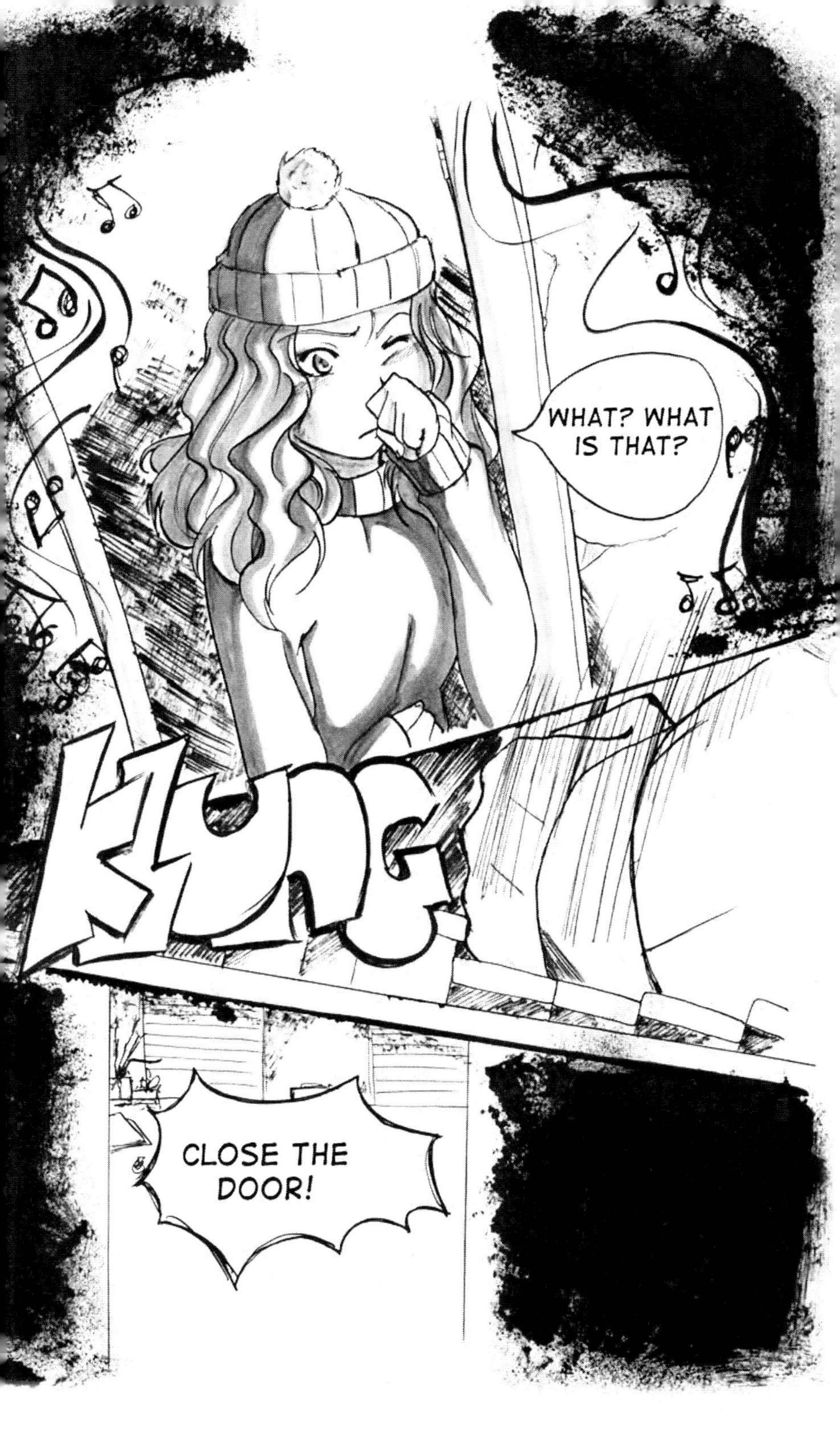
WHAT? WHAT IS THAT?
KLUNG
CLOSE THE DOOR!

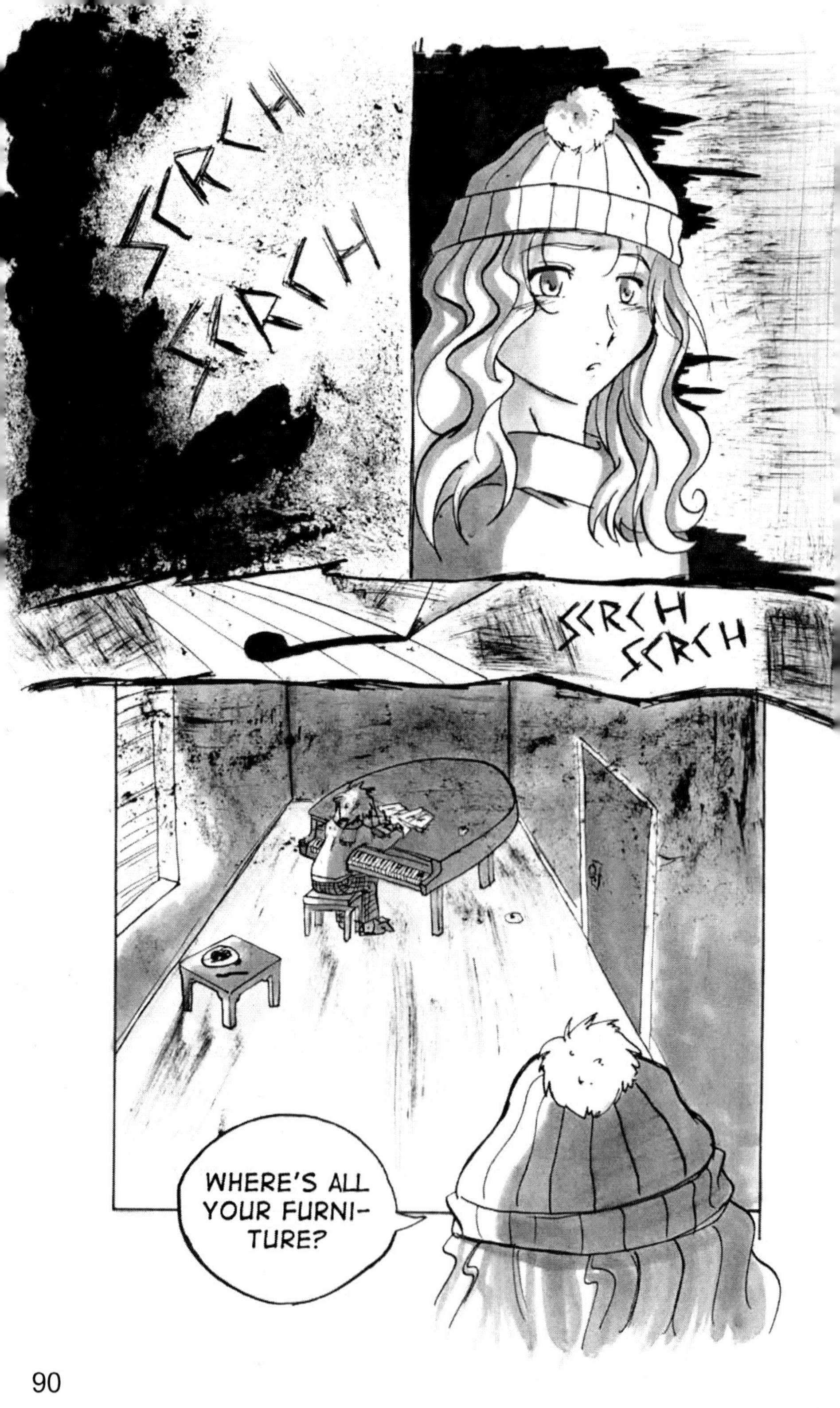
SCRCH SCRCH
SCRCH SCRCH
WHERE'S ALL YOUR FURNI-TURE?

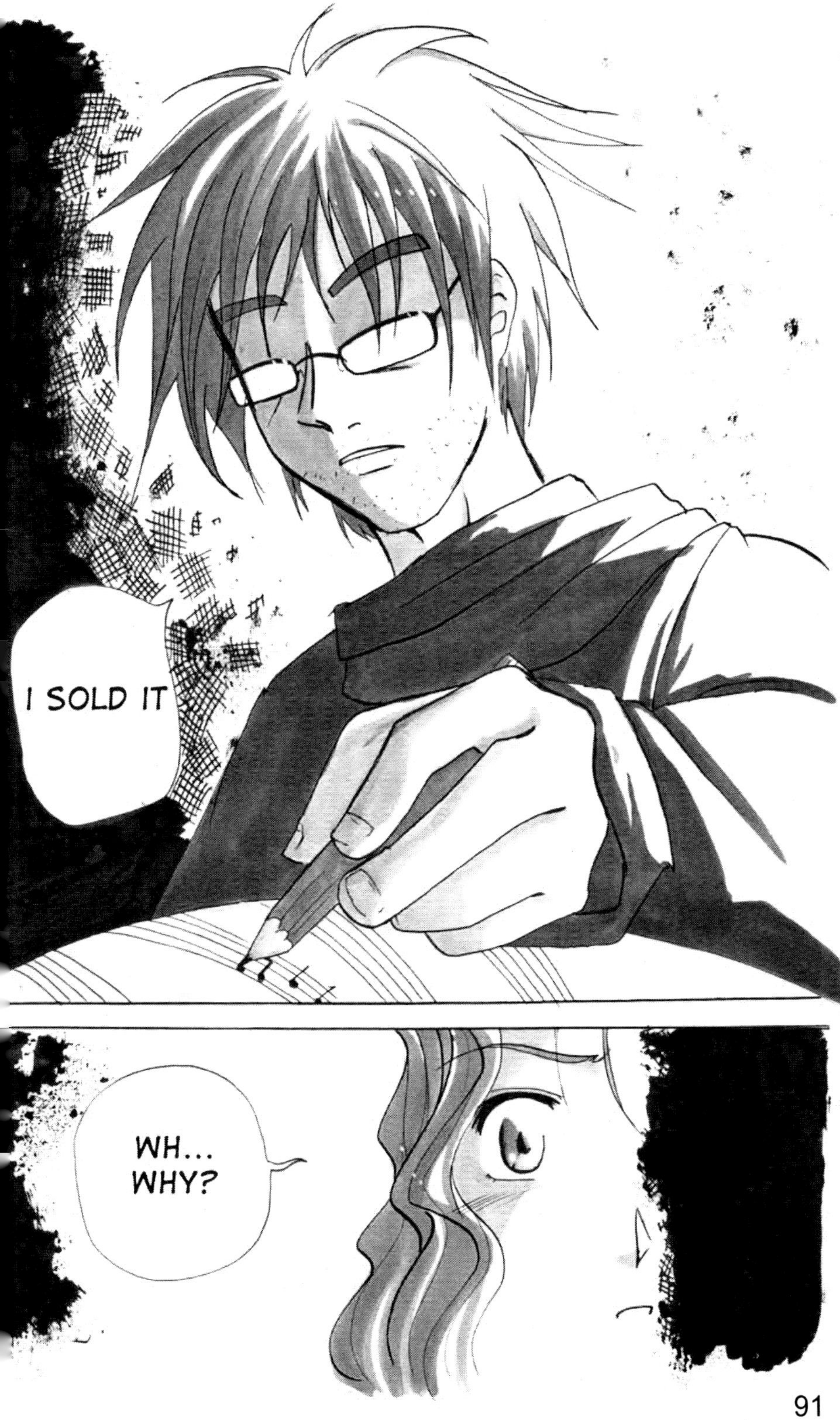
I SOLD IT
WH... WHY?

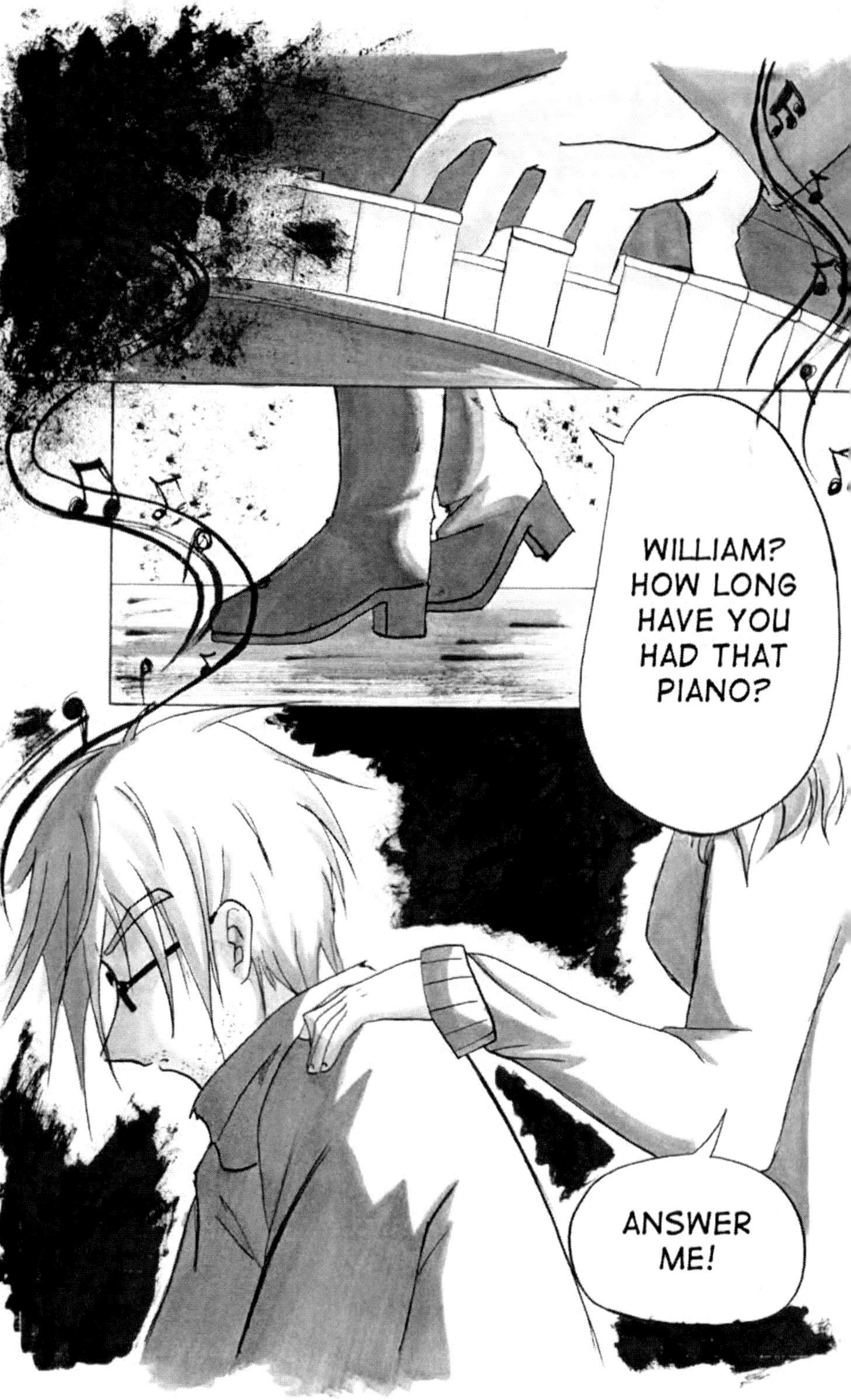
WILLIAM? HOW LONG HAVE YOU HAD THAT PIANO?
ANSWER ME!

DON'T!

JUST... DON'T
I'VE BEEN PLAYING... PLAYING THIS SONG... OVER AND OVER.
I CAN'T GET TO THE END. EVERY TIME I PLAY IT, IT SOUNDS DECAYED.
EVENTU-ALLY, IT ROTS YOU KNOW.
EVERY SONG ROTS...

ITS STENCH...
BECOMES UNBEARABLE.
YOU HIT ME... WILLIAM? HOW COULD YOU?
SHHH

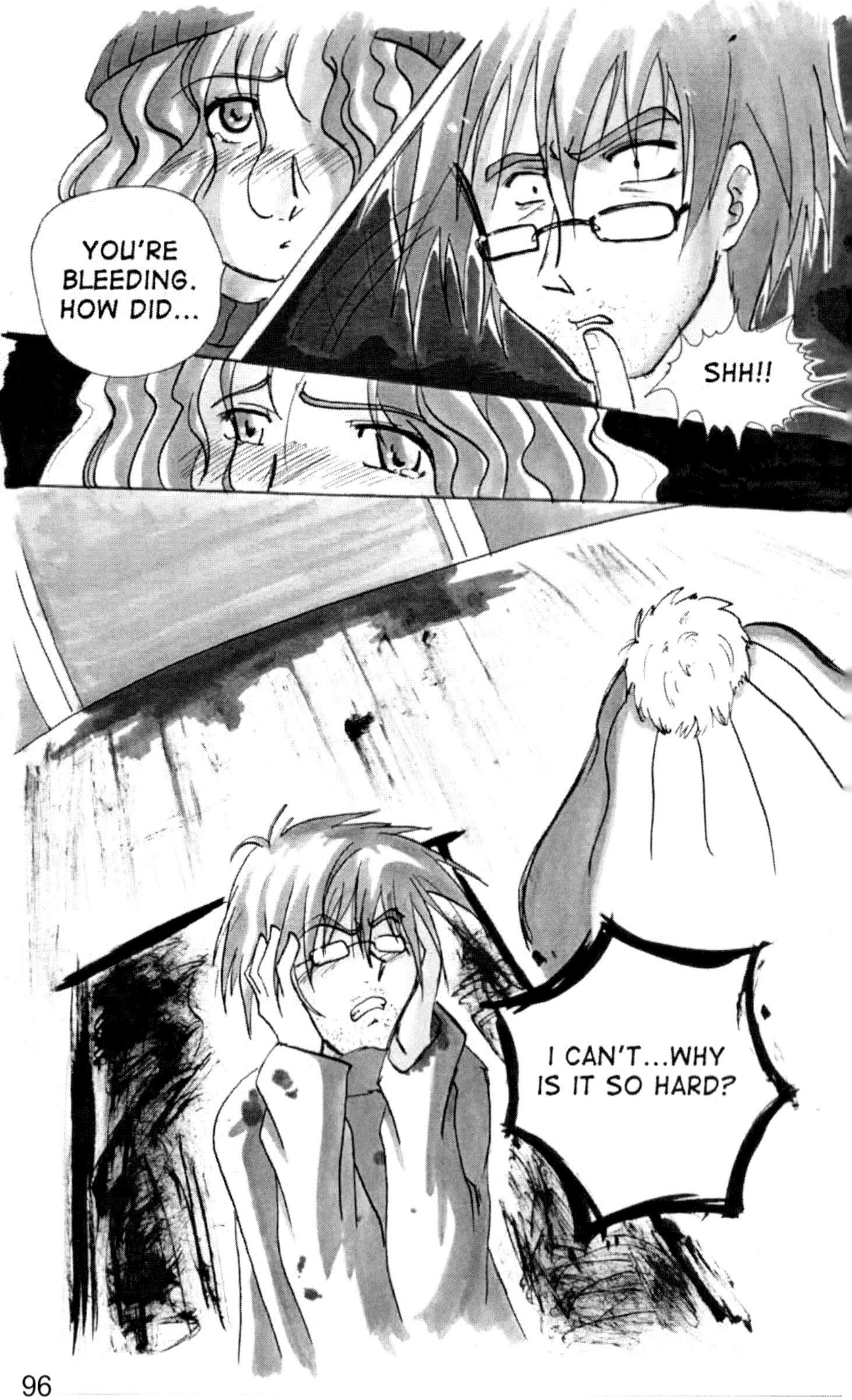
YOU'RE BLEEDING. HOW DID...
SHH!!
I CAN'T...WHY IS IT SO HARD?

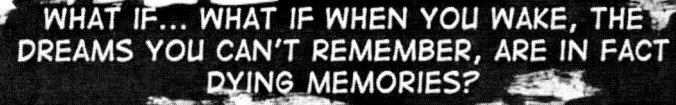

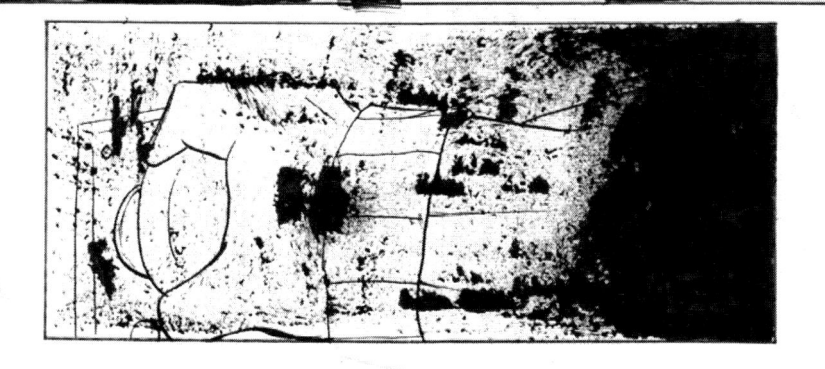

WHAT IF EVERYTHING YOU'RE FOCUSSED ON IS TOO FAR OUT OF REACH?

WHAT IF... WHAT IF WHEN YOU WAKE, THE DREAMS YOU CAN'T REMEMBER, ARE IN FACT DYING MEMORIES?

WILL YOU JUST ACCEPT IT, THINKING "I'LL STICK WITH WHAT IT IS I SEE"?

OR WILL IT END YOU?

I SAID... DON'T!

HU
HU
HU
I NEVER TOLD YOU THIS BEFORE *PANT* BUT I FOUND YOU MEDIOCRE. BUT NOW... YOU INSPIRE ME.

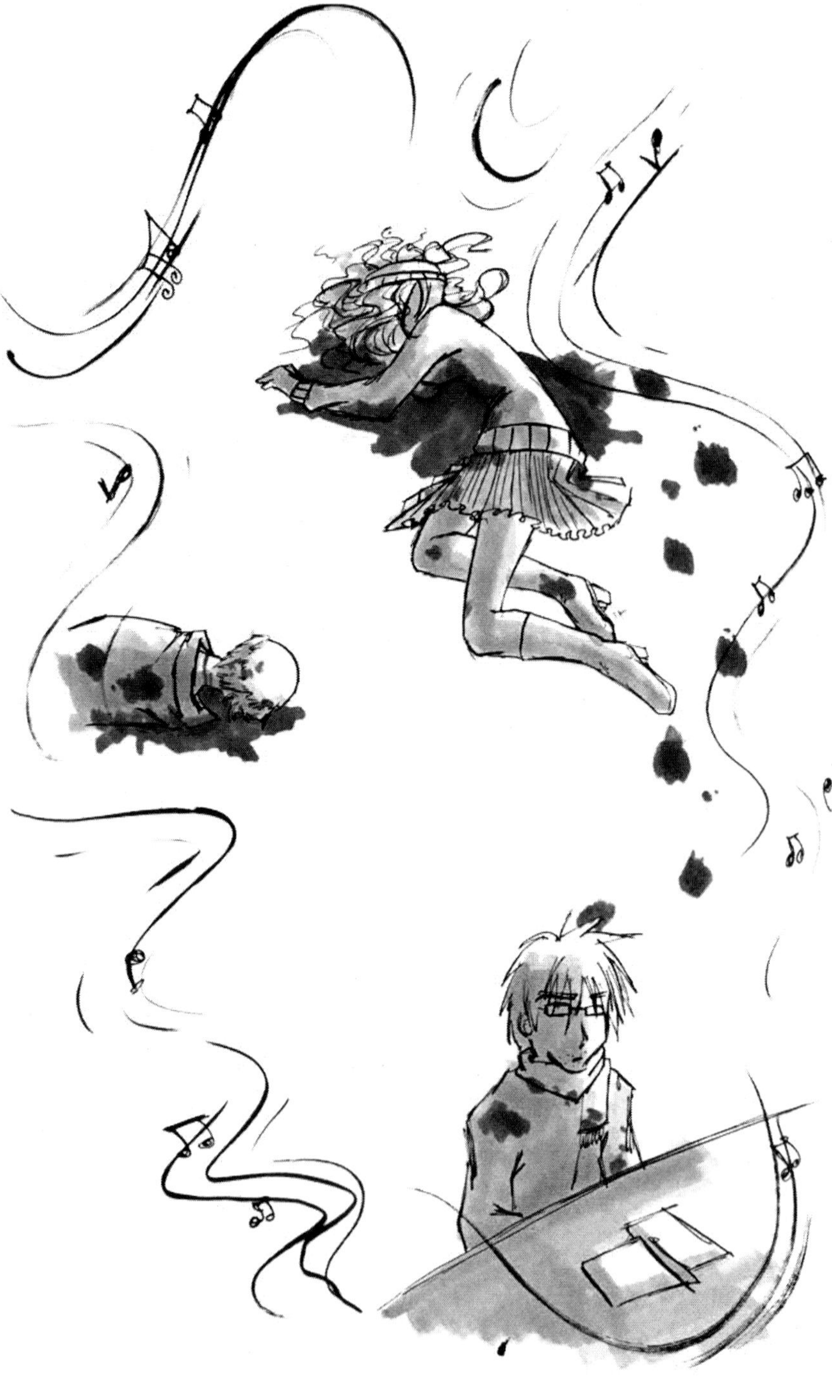

I FINALLY HAVE MY ENDING.

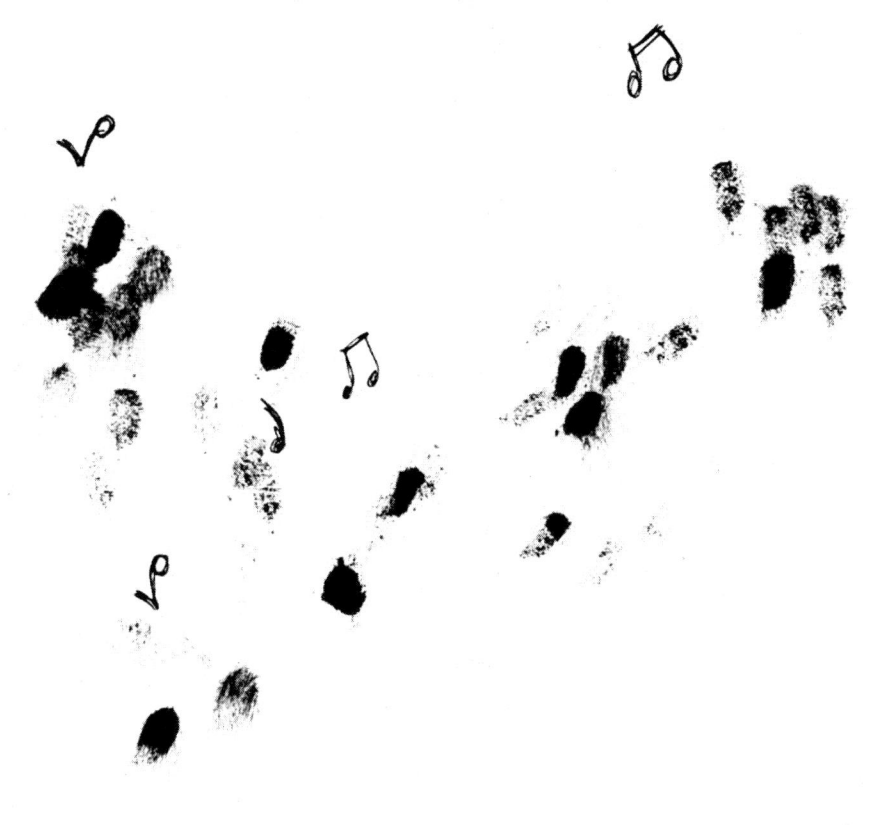

super*brother

story and art by
selina dean

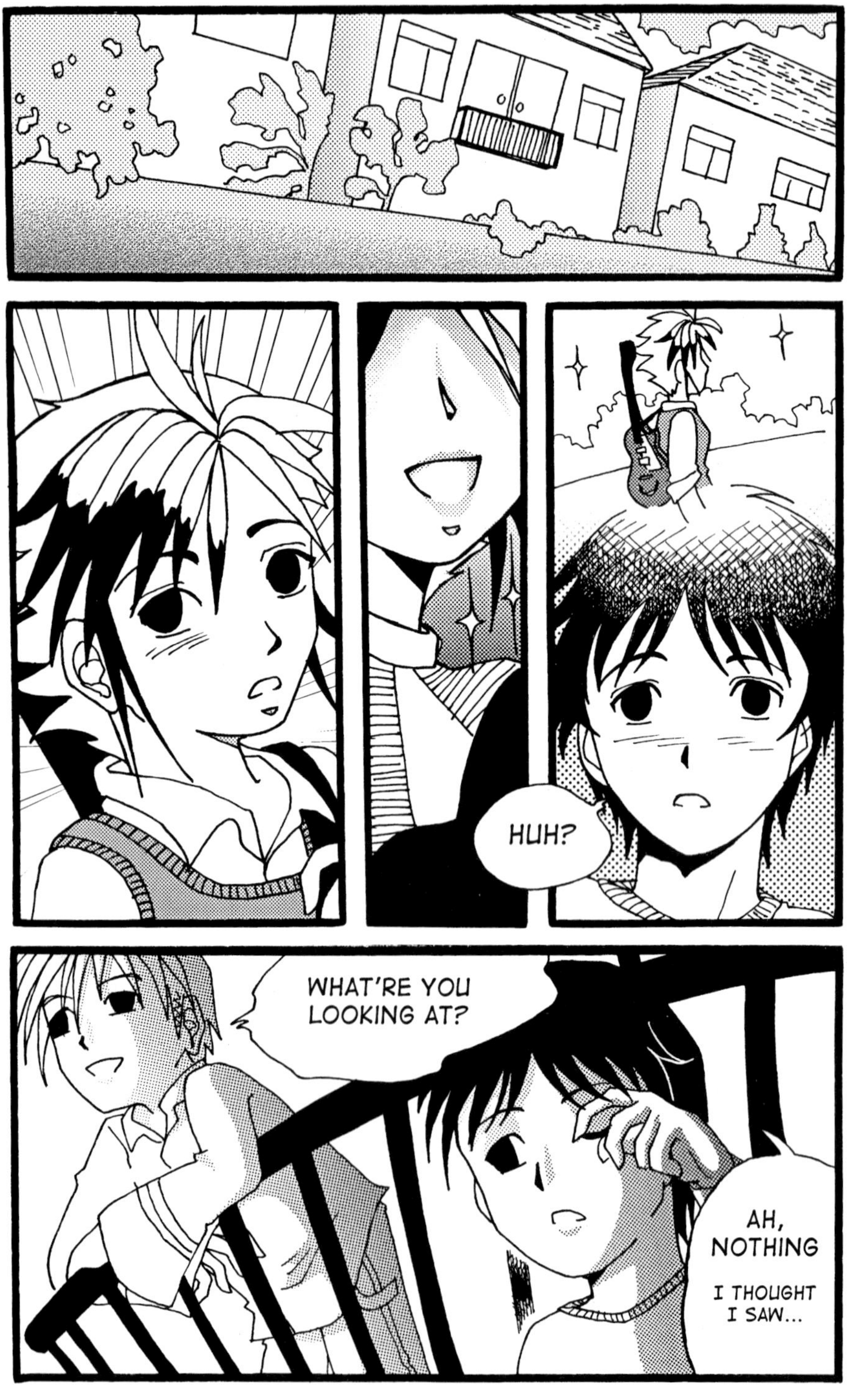
HUH?
WHAT'RE YOU LOOKING AT?
AH, NOTHING
I THOUGHT I SAW...

HEY, IT'S THAT GIRL FROM SCHOOL!
YOU KNOW? THE TEACHER WAS MOANING AT HER FOR CARRYING HER GUITAR
OH, HER
WHAT ARE YOU PLAYING?
YOU'RE RUINING MY CONCENTRATION
HER GUITAR IS SO WEIRD. IT ONLY HAS ONE STRING...
I DIED!!!
AH, BAD LUCK
YOU'RE NOT EVEN LISTENING!

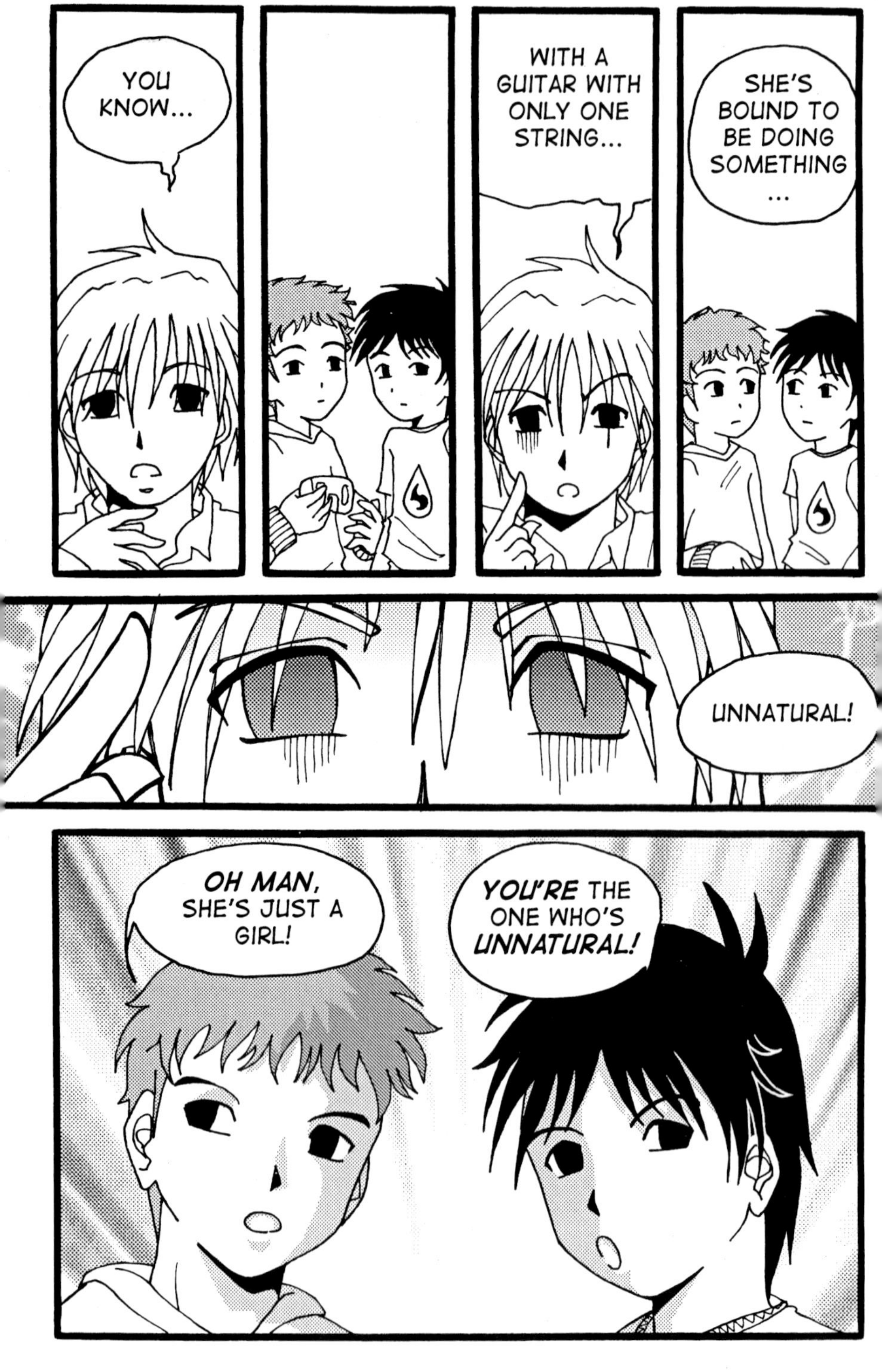
YOU KNOW...
WITH A GUITAR WITH ONLY ONE STRING...
SHE'S BOUND TO BE DOING SOMETHING ...
UNNATURAL!
OH MAN, SHE'S JUST A GIRL!
YOU'RE THE ONE WHO'S UNNATURAL!

HEH!

WELL, IF YOU'RE SO SURE...

SHE WON'T MIND YOU ASKING ABOUT HER GUITAR

THIS IS SO STUPID

GO! BEFORE SHE ESCAPES!

SHOVE

WHY ME?

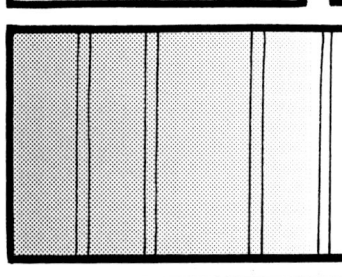

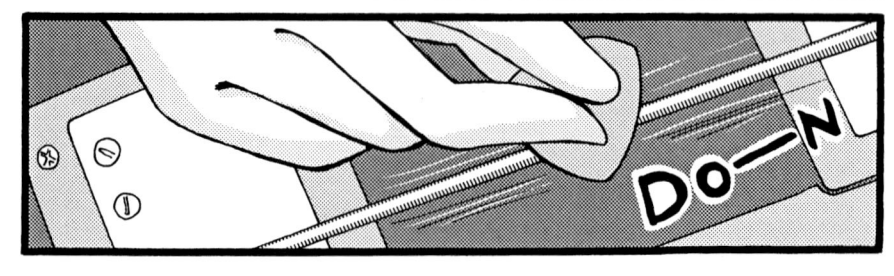

AH, WHERE DID SHE GO?

DO—N

S-SHE'S...

GONE!

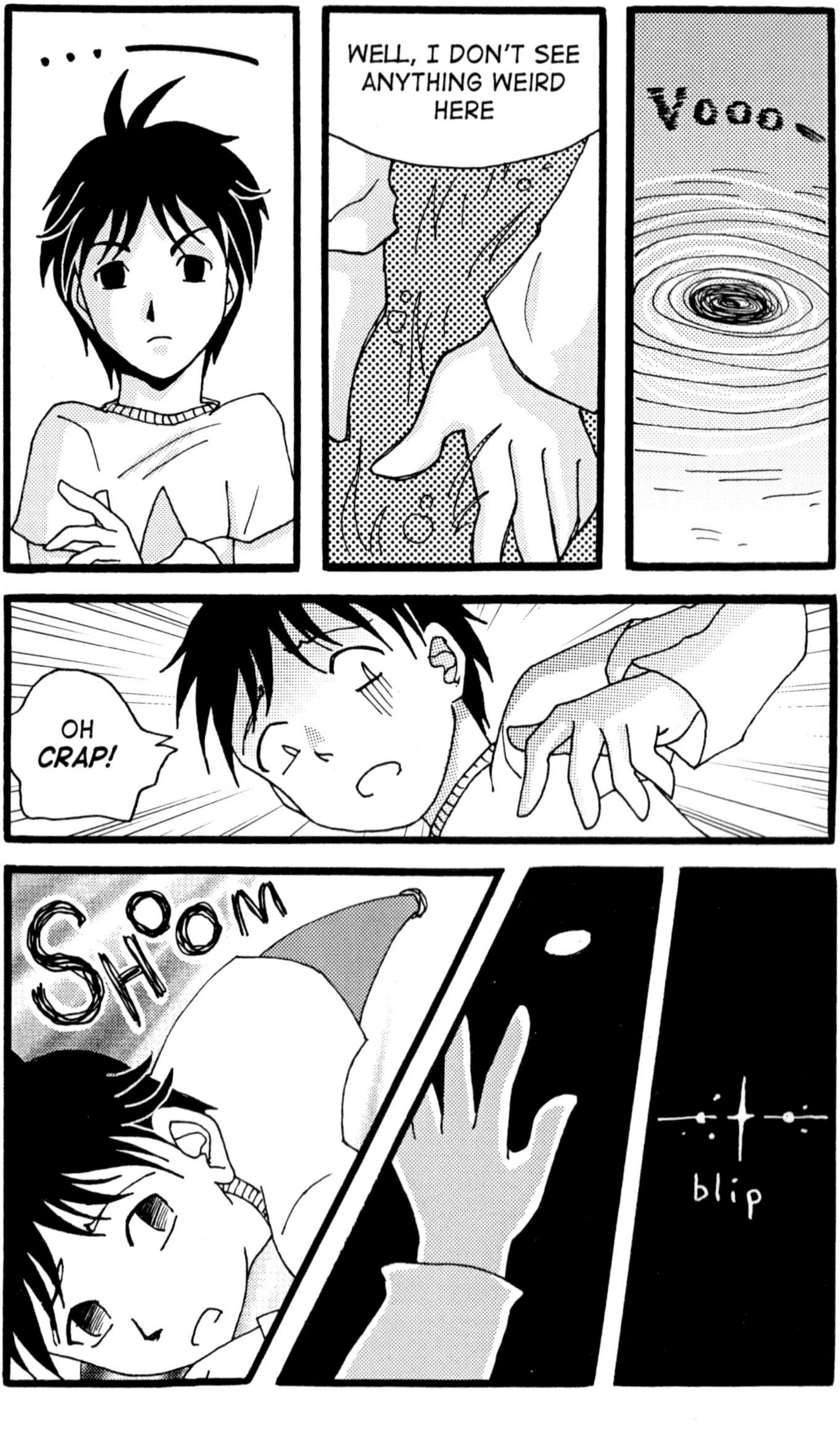
...—
WELL, I DON'T SEE ANYTHING WEIRD HERE
Vooo-
OH CRAP!
SHOOM
blip

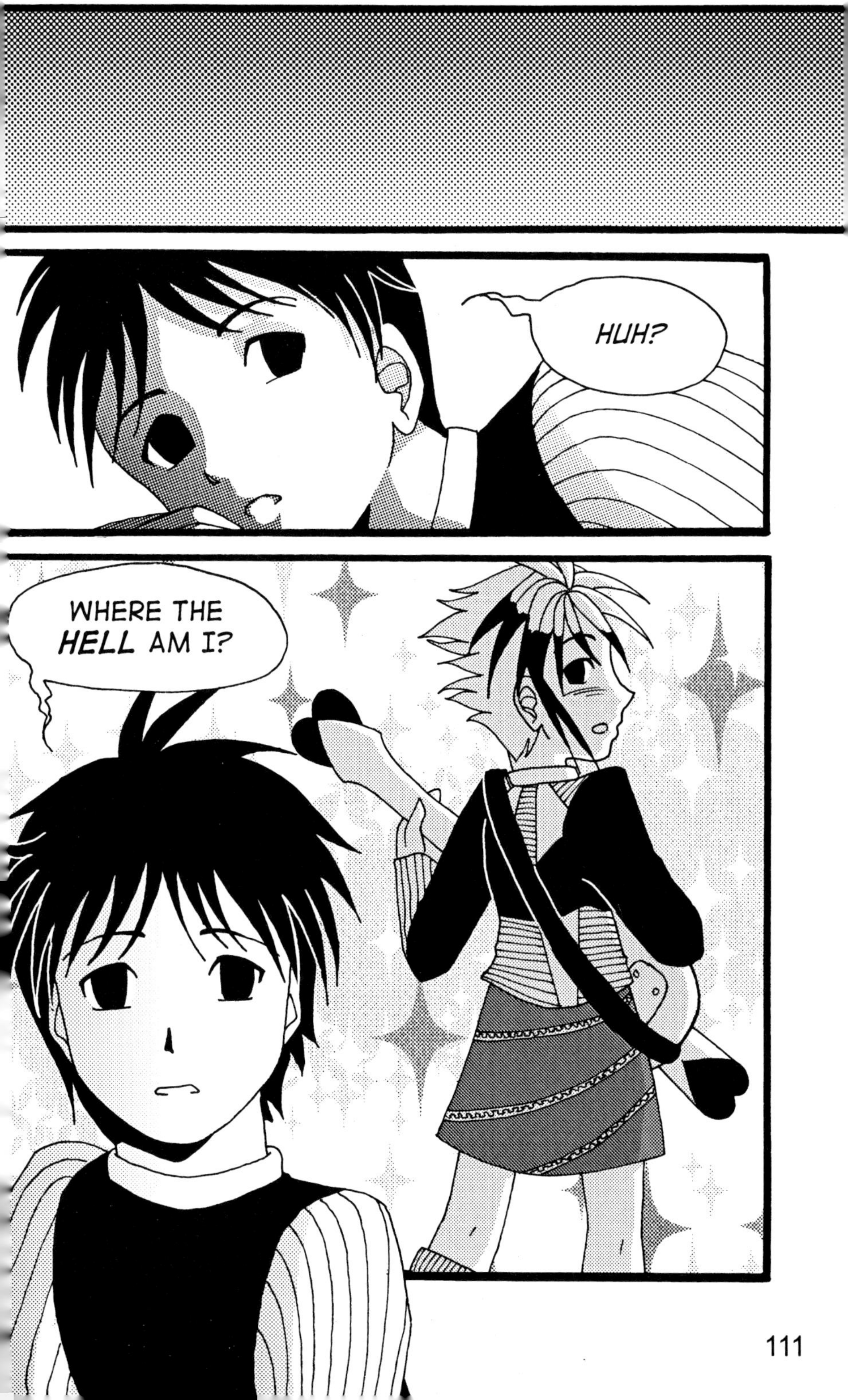
HUH?
WHERE THE HELL AM I?

HOW DID YOU...
AAH!
-SKEEE-
...A GOOD FIGHT, BUT SHE WAS THE UNDERDOG
THIS IS...
I WONDER HOW THIS MYSTERIOUS NEW CHALLENGER WILL FARE

...SOME KIND OF *BATTLE!*

SO I'LL DO WHATEVER IT TAKES TO WIN!

AH! I FOR- GOT!

I CAN'T PLAY GUITAR!

HEH. WELL, WHOEVER HE IS HE LOOKS LIKE HE'S HAVING A LITTLE TROUBLE
WITH PLAYING LIKE THAT, I'M SURPRISED HE KNOWS WHICH END TO BLOW THROUGH!
HAH! WHAT'S WRONG? CAN'T YOU EVEN HANDLE THAT GIRLY GUITAR?
...
THIS IS GOING TO BE TOO EASY!

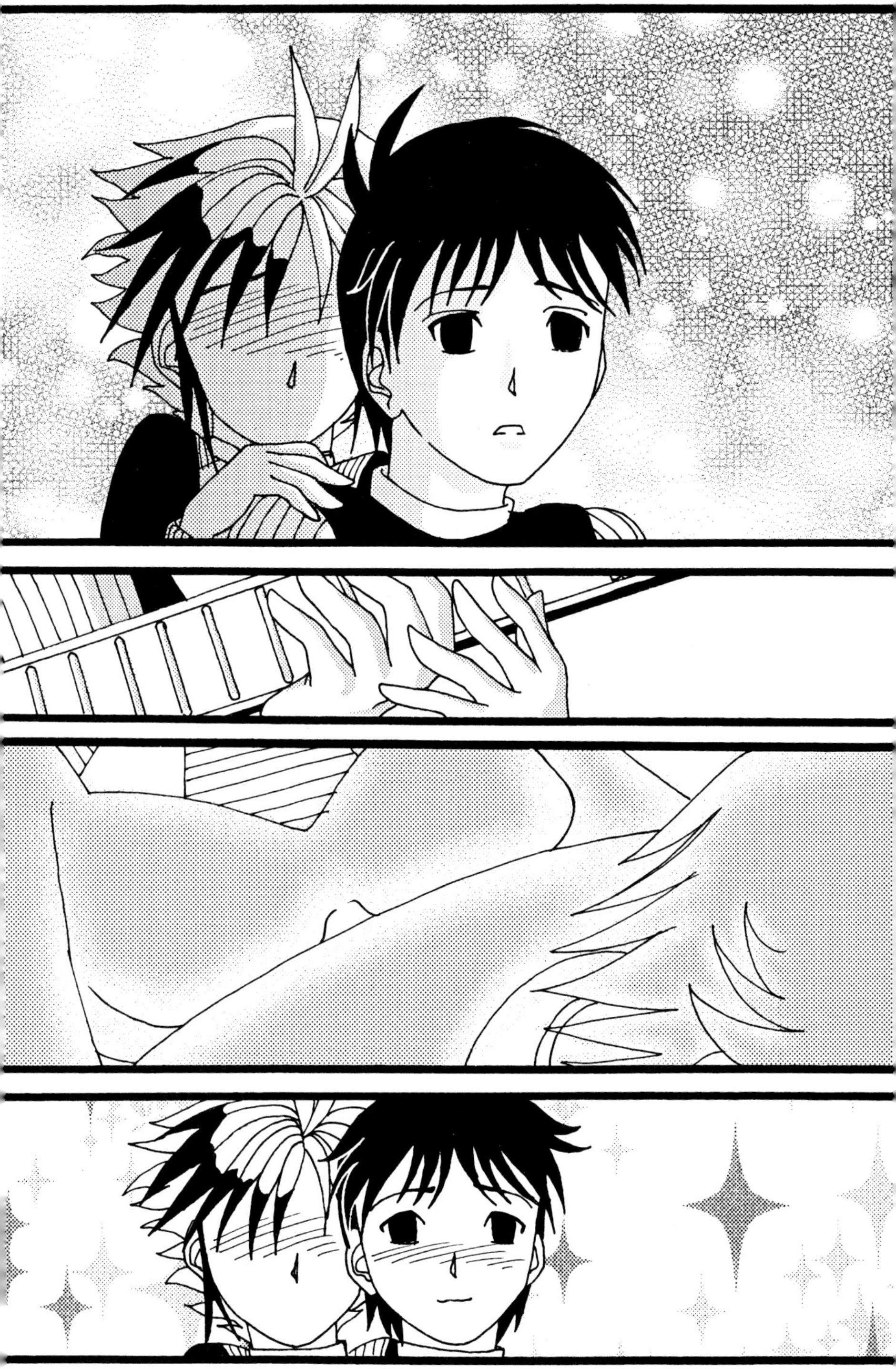

PLAY IT LIKE THIS

WOW! AN AMAZING COMEBACK AFTER A SHAKY START...

THIS WEEK'S WINNER IS *MITSUKO!*

YOU'VE BECOME A *FREAK* LIKE *HER*

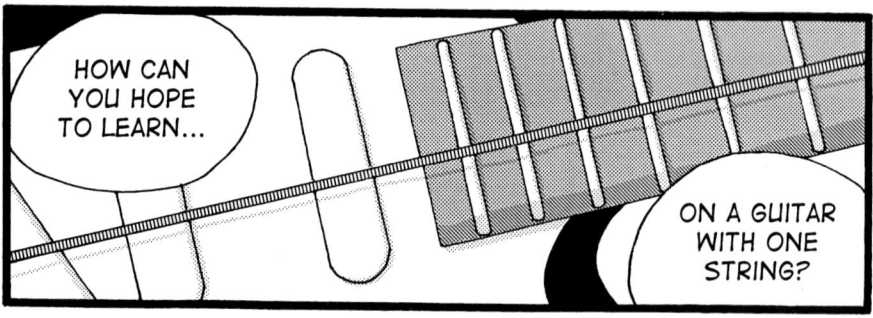

I DON'T *BELIEVE* IT!

EH?

HOW CAN YOU HOPE TO LEARN...

ON A GUITAR WITH ONE STRING?

BUT IT DOESN'T MATTER WHAT I PLAY...

ALL THAT MATTERS ...

IS HOW YOU PLAY IT

THE END

Transmutation

Artwork by **Vanessa Wells**, story by **Selina Dean**

ALL MY LIFE I'VE WANTED TO BECOME A BEAUTIFUL BUTTERFLY..
..BUT ALL I AM IS AN UGLY MOTH.

COME ONE, COME ALL, LADIES AND GENTLEMEN TO EXPERINENCE THE MIRACLE CURE.
WHAT DOES IT CURE, YOU ASK..
..IT CURES UNHAPPINESS..

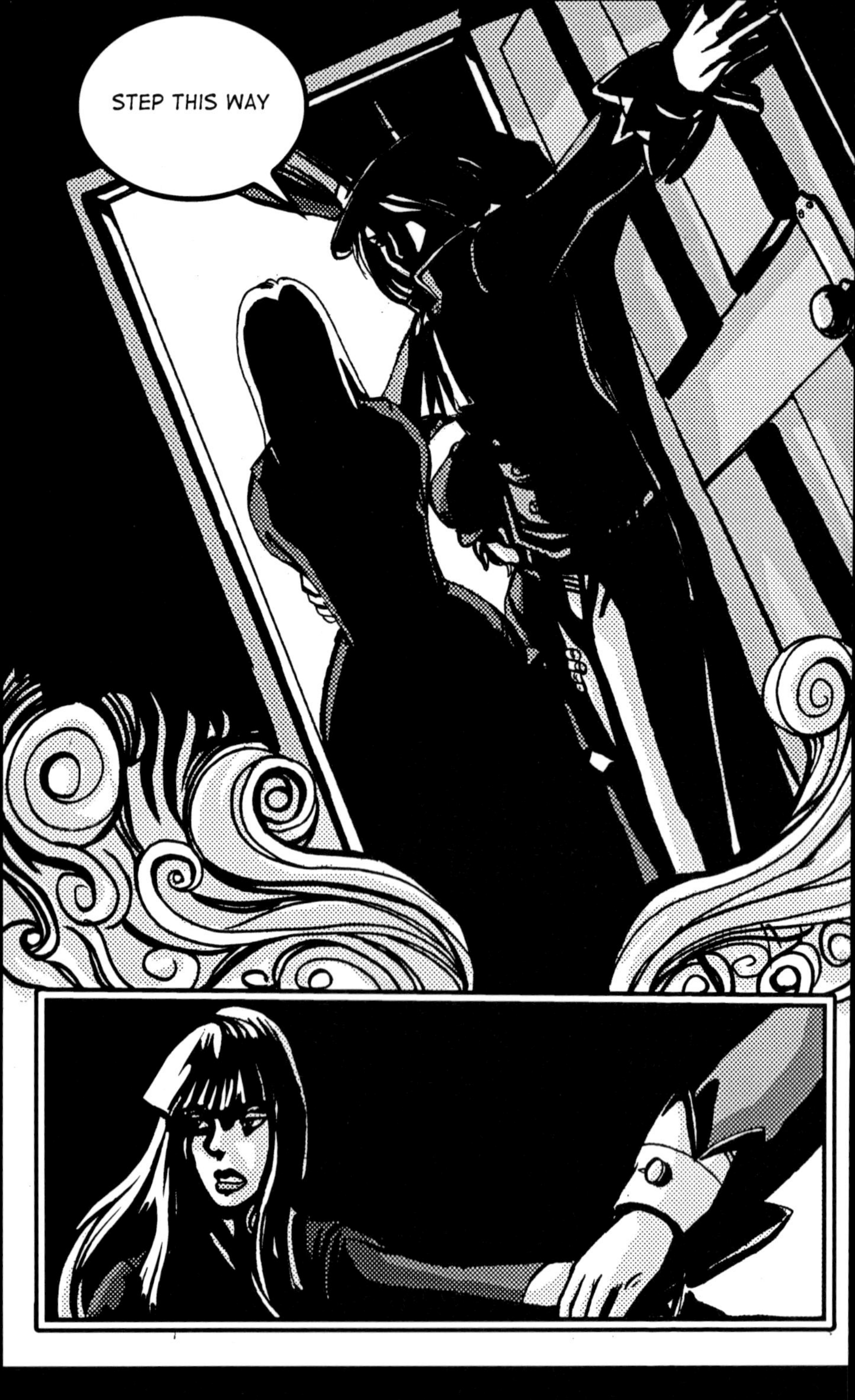
STEP THIS WAY

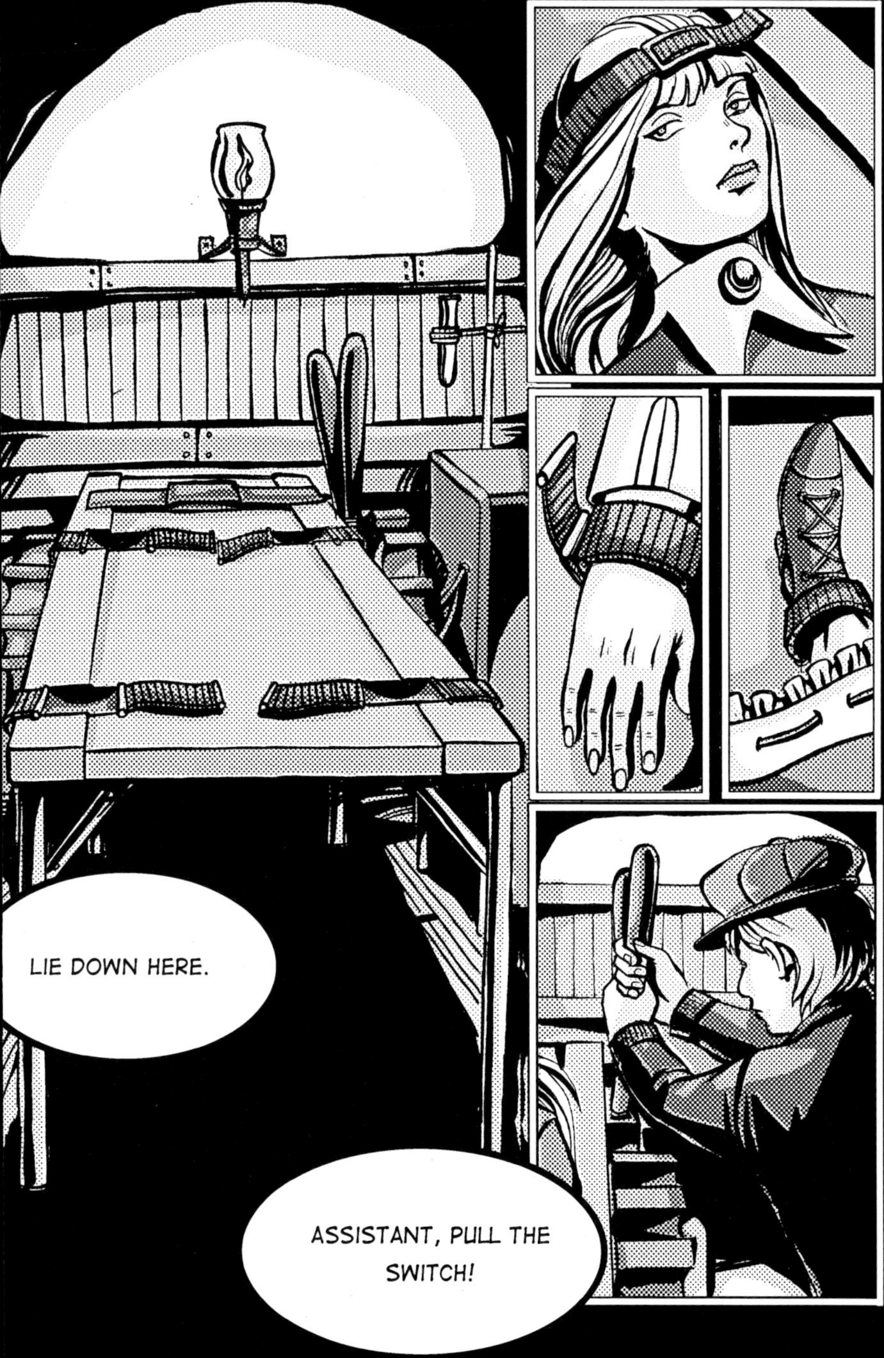
LIE DOWN HERE.
ASSISTANT, PULL THE SWITCH!

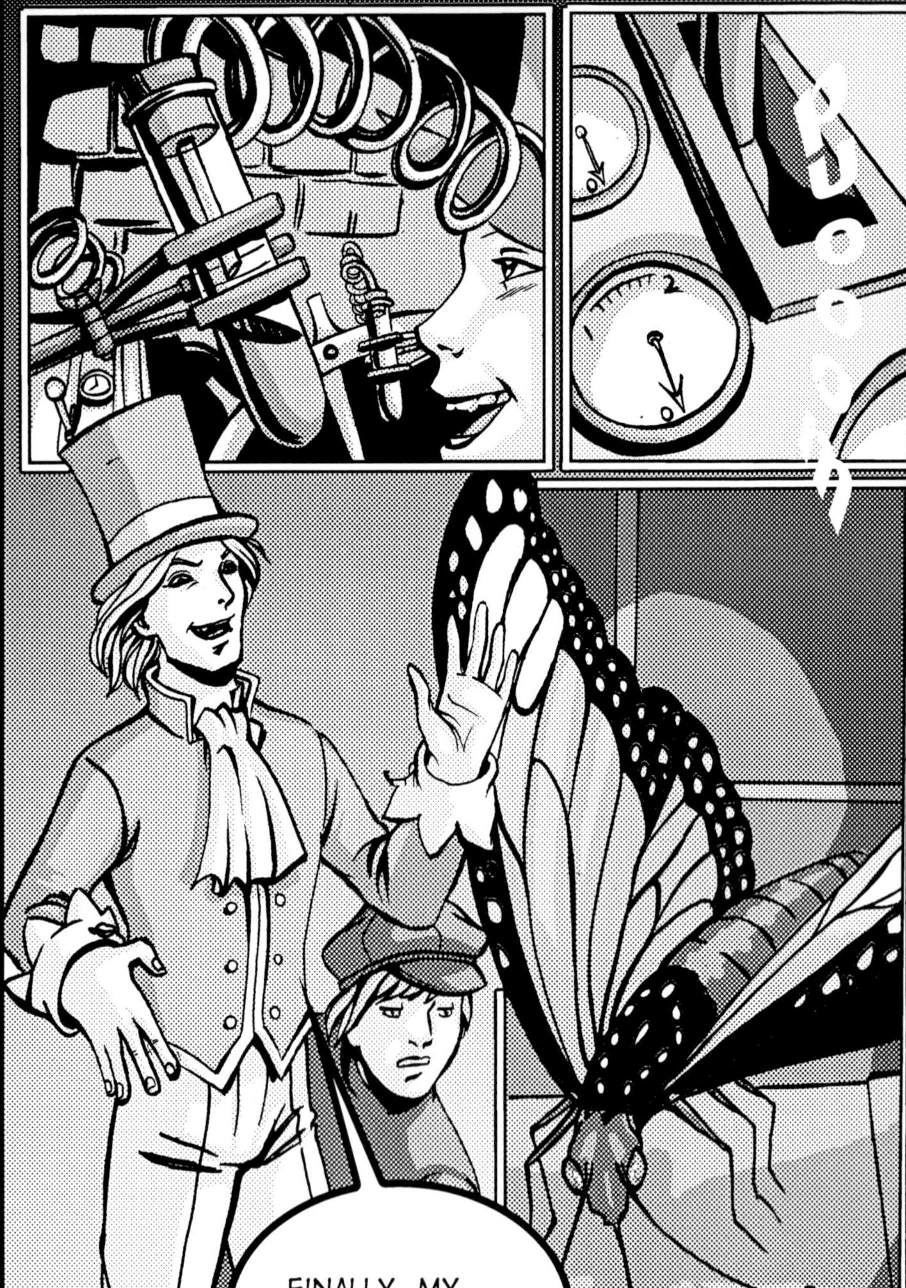
FINALLY, MY MACHINE WORKS!!

about us

Sam Brown
http://www.revolutionbaby.com
Sam Brown (a.k.a. Subi) is a world-renowned Arctic explorer (by bicycle), editor of the Egyptian Book of the Dead, and the first man on Venus. Or at least that's what his entry at Wikipedia would say if it didn't keep getting edited back. He is, however, genuinely a founding member of Sweatdrop and creator of *'Revolution Baby'* and *'Binkan Shounen Kurodzu Kuri'* (with Mary Beaird).

Hayden Scott-Baron
http://www.deadpanda.com
dock@deadpanda.com
Hayden Scott-Baron (a.k.a. Dock) is a professional video-games artist and loves to draw manga in his free time. *'Two Halves: Blue Skies'* is a comedy tale with a splash of parody, quite a diversion from his usual drama-themed stories. Hayden has designed characters for video-games, clothing and magazines, and is also the author of various how-to books on the topic of drawing manga.

Rik Nicol
http://www.hamstercurry.com/
Rik Nicol is a London-based illustrator and graphic designer whose work frequently explores the stylistic elements of 'disposable' pop culture, particularly that of the far east. He has worked on comics, animations, games and websites among other creative fields but regularly undertakes new mediums with which to experiment and expand his skill-set. Rik produced the piece *'Quest for Chenezzar'* with a combination of Painter (IX) and Photoshop (CS2).

Sarah Burgess
http://denji.deviantart.com
Sarah Burgess is a budding artist currently studying at art college, and has contributed to the anthology with *'Unmade Melody'*. She is the artist for various comics from Sweatdrop, including two other anthology pieces and the longer-running series, *'Those Who Can Dance On The Feathers'*. Sarah also has a shoujo style webcomic, *'Bento Best Friend'*, which can be read on her website.

Hannah Saunders
http://www.wanderingmuse.co.uk
Hannah Saunders (a.k.a. Wandering Muse) is currently a student at college, and the creator of Sweatdrop shoujo title *'Nimbus Base'*. Her contribution to the anthology was *'Angel's Game: Steel Destrier'*, for which she was the artist. For more of her artwork, please visit her website.

Laura Watton
http://www.laurawatton.co.uk
Laura Watton is one of the founding members of Sweatdrop Studios. Her main title is *'Biomecha'* but has also created numerous other titles and has contributed to several Sweatdrop anthologies. She was also the editor for the anthology, *'Stardust'*. Her contribution, *'Steaming'*, was co-written by Aleister Kelman. She is currently working on *'Biomecha 6'*, *'Reluctant Soldier Princess Nami'* and a collected *'Boiled Spoons'*. Laura was also a winner of the 2006 Neo Magazine manga competition and hopes to continue to draw as many manga-styled comics as possible!

Stephanie Drewett
http://yan-ryu.deviantart.com/
Stephanie Drewett (a.k.a. Yan-ryu) has been a Sweatdrop member since March 2005. Since joining she has produced a short story called *'Glomp'* as well as starting her ongoing series *'Mango Milkshake'*. In the relatively short time she has been a member she has also produced a daughter, Poppy, who has taken up a lot of valuable drawing time, but still managed to finish her first anthology contribution.

Selina Dean
http://www.noddingcat.net
Selina has more comics than can be mentioned here, but her two main series for now are *'Fantastic Cat'* and *'Fantasma'*. She has contributed to various articles and books on drawing manga, and two of her comics are published in *'The Mammoth Book of Best New Manga'*. She enjoyed working with Vanessa on *'Transmutation'*, and taking the role of evil writer for a while!

Vanessa Wells
http://www.vanessa.withbits.com
Vanessa loves doing comics as it keeps her out of trouble. Her scribblings are somewhere between Manga and Western style, and she's happy enough about that as she loves both styles. She's currently penning a series called *'Shrouded'*, an epic adventure tale. She gives many thanks to Selina for the cool story to draw.

Fehed Said
http://www.sixkillerbunnies.com
Fehed Said is proud to have been part of this exciting project and has had stories featured in Sweatdrop anthologies in the past. Other Sweatdrop works are *'co_OKiE'*, *'Faded & Torn'* and *'The Politics of Tears'*, with artwork by Shari Chankhamma, Keds and Emma Vieceli respectively. Recent titles by Fehed (with artwork from Shari) to have been picked up are the upcoming *'The Clarence Principle'* from Slave Labor Graphics and *'The Healing'* featured in *'The Mammoth Book of Best New Manga'*. Fehed has some exciting Sweatdrop titles lined up for 2007. Keep an eye out.

> WHAT IF EVERYTHING YOU'RE FOCUSSED ON IS TOO FAR OUT OF REACH?

Mary Beaird
http://www.diyhamstercraft.com
Mary Beaird is one of Sweatdrop's two writers. Her current titles are *'Binkan Shounen Kurodzu Kuri'*, in partnership with Subi, and *'Tetraspace'*, a series of short stories featuring different artists. Her third comic, *'Elephant Elephant Hippo Rhino…?'* is her only solo effort. Her featured story is *'Angel's Game: Steel Destrier'*, with artwork by Hannah Saunders.

> …THERE'S SOMETHING WORSE UP AHEAD!!

Thank you for reading!
We're all proud to be part of this anthology, and hope you enjoyed reading it. If you liked what you read here, you can find more work by these artists at **www.sweatdrop.com**

SEE THE STORY FROM A NEW PERSPECTIVE!

*There are always **two sides** to every story, but it's not often you get to experience **both**!*

"Pink is for girls" re-tells the tales from "Blue is for boys" but with a very different emphasis.

See the same characters from a completely new perspective, or even read stories that take place simultaneously alongside one you've already read. Protagonists become antagonists, antagonists become love interests, and some characters transform into something else entirely.

Sweatdrop Studios presents a unique experiment in comic form, intertwining yet also defining male and female sensibilities in manga.

AN ELEGANT SWEATDROP ANTHOLOGY FOR LADIES

PINK IS FOR GIRLS

sweatdrop studios

WITH ARTWORK BY:
- EMMA VIECELI
- SONIA LEONG
- MORAG LEWIS
- ALEISTER KELMAN
- REBECCA BURGESS
- NIKI HUNTER
- WING YUN MAN
- JACQUELINE KWONG
- CARRIE DEAN

ADDITIONAL WRITING BY:
- FEHED SAID
- MARY BEAIRD
- SELINA DEAN

AND FOREWORD BY:
- HELEN McCARTHY

A 'SHOJO MANGA' APPROACH TO NINE SHORT STORIES

PINK IS FOR GIRLS  ↔ BLUE IS FOR BOYS

AVAILABLE NOW FROM SWEATDROP STUDIOS!

OTHER SWEATDROP ANTHOLOGY TITLES

Cold Sweat & Tears

A Sweatdrop Anthology about Human Emotion. This book compiles ten short stories from previously released collections 'Love, Sweat & Tears' and 'Cold Sweat', along with bonus artwork and information, in perfect bound format. Ten gripping tales that tread the line between love and fear.

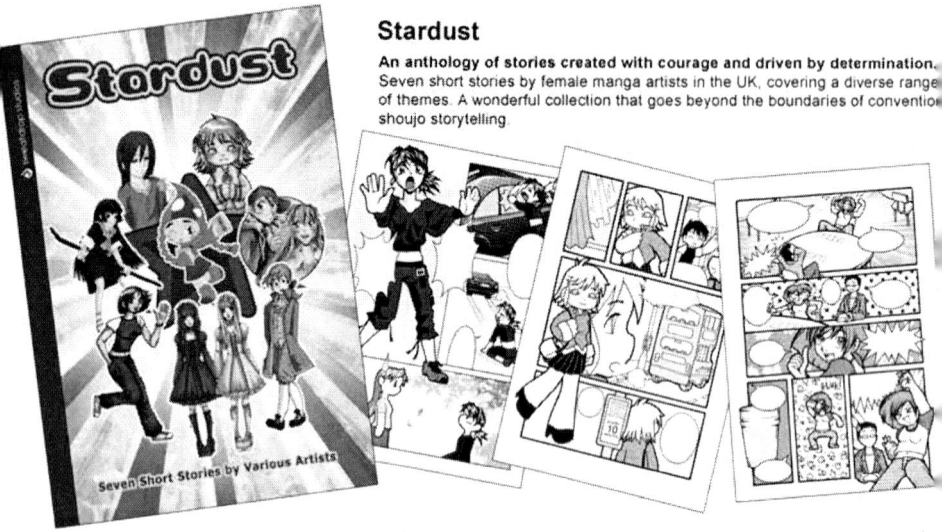

Stardust

An anthology of stories created with courage and driven by determination. Seven short stories by female manga artists in the UK, covering a diverse range of themes. A wonderful collection that goes beyond the boundaries of conventional shoujo storytelling.

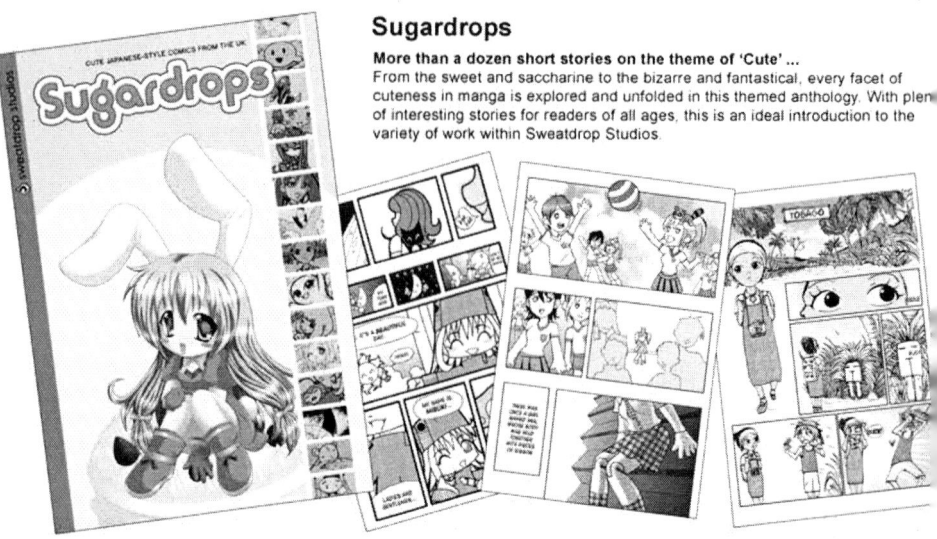

Sugardrops

More than a dozen short stories on the theme of 'Cute' ...
From the sweet and saccharine to the bizarre and fantastical, every facet of cuteness in manga is explored and unfolded in this themed anthology. With plenty of interesting stories for readers of all ages, this is an ideal introduction to the variety of work within Sweatdrop Studios.

MORE UK-MANGA BOOKS FROM SWEATDROP!

Fantastic Cat volume 1, by Selina Dean

Flying cats and people who fall from the sky!
Oskar loses his memory, but gains some friends. It's a shame they're just a little strange... No matter how far you run (or should that be fly?) your past will always catch up to you.

Looking for the Sun volume 1 & 2, by Morag Lewis

Kite is looking for the sun. Why? Because it's lost...
Somewhere among the myriad worlds there is one which has lost its sun. All the hydrogen's still there at the centre of the solar system, where the sun used to be, but the world is in darkness and will eventually die if something is not done.

Revolution Baby volume 1, by Sam Brown (Subi)

ANIME FANS RULE THE COUNTRY ... but it's not the perfect world we imagined In the midst of the chaos of counterrevolution, idol singer meets bunny girl and they plunge into a maelstrom of music, cliché, students, violent cops, tight bodysuits, great big f--k-off robots, lightspeed martial arts and panties. ONLY A DEUS EX MACHINA ENDING CAN SAVE THEM NOW!

catalogue

Title	Author
Anamnesis 1	Subi
Artifaxis 1-5	Morag Lewis
Ashcom 1-3	Various
Attic	Dock
Binkan Shounen Kurodzu Kuri 1-2	Subi
Biomecha 4-5	Laura Watton
Black Cat, White Cat	Selina Dean
Cold Sweat And Tears	Various
Cookie	Fred and Shari
Cyber Crush	Joanna Zhou
Cyborg Butterfly	Sonia Leong
Distant Thunder 1-2	Foxy
Dragon Heir 3-5	Emma Vieceli
Duel Class vol.1	Ken Hoang
Elephant, Elephant, Hippo, Rhino...?	Mary Beaird
Falling Short	Keds
Fantasma 1-3	Selina Dean
Fantastic Cat 2.1	Selina Dean
Fantastic Cat vol 1	Selina Dean
Glomp	Stephanie Drewett
Harajuku Zoo	Joanna Zhou
Illusional Beauty 1-4	Bex
Jar	Selina Dean
Kaia 1-2	Carrie Dean
Killer Cake	Marubelle.S
Kindred Spirits 2-3	Keds
Looking For The Sun 1-15	Morag Lewis
Looking For The Sun vol. 1-2	Morag Lewis
Mango Milkshake 1	Stephanie Drewett
Nimbus Base 1	Hannah Saunders
Once Upon A Time... 1-3	Sonia Leong
Revolution Baby 6-9	Subi
Revolution Baby vol.1	Subi
Snails Don't Have Friends	Selina Dean
Stardust	Various
Sugardrops	Various
Sunshine Bully	Laura Watton
Squishy-chan's Adventure	Laura Watton
Tetraspace 1	Morag Lewis, Mary Beaird
Those Who Can Dance On The Feathers 1-3	Denji
White Cat	Selina Dean

available now, from
sweatdrop
ORIGINAL UK MANGA STUDIOS
www.sweatdrop.com